Author & Design

Steven Trustrum

Cover Art & Interior Illustrations

David Hamilton

Additional Illustration

V Shane

Logo

Gerry Alvarez

Interior Colours

Steven Trustrum

http://www.misfit-studios.com

Product Identity

The following items are hereby identified as Product Identity, as defined in the Open Gaming License version 1.0a, Section 1(e), and are not Open Content. All trademarks, registered trademarks, proper names (characters, artifacts, places, etc.), artwork and trade dress.

Declaration of Open Game Content

All text pertaining to game mechanics and statistics, along with the class names, are declared Open Game Content. All items subject to the definition of Product Identity (see previous) are the property of Misfit Studios™ and cannot be used without written permission.

Table of Contents

Chapter 1

Introduction

In 2005, **Misfit Studios** released the original *Superior Synergy: Fantasy* for the 3.5 OGL rules. The product quickly became one of our best, most consistent sellers. Customers voiced their enjoyment of how the product took the concept of Skill Synergy and made it more dynamic and expansive, allowing for benefits that went well beyond a mere +2 bonus. Customers also responded well to the seemingly logical extension of Skill Synerg by permitting feats to work together in a similar manner in the new game mechanic, Feat Synergy. With the decline of the 3.5 rules and rising popularity of **The Pathfinder Roleplaying Game**'s mechanics, which dropped Skill Synergy entirely as something that imbalanced gameplay, it seemed there was an ideal opportunity to revisit the product and see what could be done with it.

Rather than merely change the effect names from the original product to match the changes made in **The Pathfinder Roleplaying Game** rules, a process that would not have addressed the latter's concerns about Skill Synergy's influence on game balance, Skill Synergy has instead been wholly redesigned. This new approach has been carried out in a way that better accommodaes game balance while acknowledging the changes made to the skill mechanics. It takes a fresh approach that improve upon the original concept while also expanding the material.

In *Superior Synergy: Fantasy PFRPG Edition*, Skill Synergy no longer represents the effects of two skills having a beneficial relationship as an increasing bonus. In other words, your Skill Synergy benefits no longer automatically get better the more ranks you have in a particular skill. The new approach operates under the assumption that nothing is taken for granted. Drawing upon secondary knowledge or talents in order to grant a synergy benefit to another skill requires effort in its own right and includes a degree of uncertainty. Indeed, trying to draw upon your skills for the purpose of Skill Synergy may even result in making things worse rather than better!

As for Feat Synergy, a bounty of new material has been added, more than doubling the Feat Synergy effects presented in the original, 2005 product. The revised edition also introduces three entirely new synergy concepts: that of Class Synergy (multiclassing allows abilities from different classes to work together), Magic Synergy (spells working together towards new effects), and Craft Synergy (the relationships between skills, feats, and class abilities allowing for interesting crafting results.) On top of everything, all content has been better organized and clarified for ease of use and reference.

With *Superior Synergy: Fantasy PFRPG Edition*, players must no longer just think about which feats to choose for their character and where to allocate skill points upon gaining a new experience level. Now, you also have to think about how all those choices may come together in a web of interaction that can allow for new and unexpected results via synergy.

By no means are the Synergy Effects presented within meant to represent the entire span of possibility. If you think there is a relationship between two related game mechanics that should reasonably have a synergy relationship, by all means write it up. Class Synergy and Feat Synergy are especially likely to have Synergy Effects not covered in this book. Use what is presented here to come up with your own ideas.

That being said, welcome the return of synergy to your game.

Chapter 2

Skill Synergy

hen **the Pathfinder Roleplaying Game** came along, it removed Skill Synergy because the designers believed it had negative repercussions on game balance and pacing. It seems the designers agreed with complaints many players had regarding the synergy game mechanic, as presented in the 3.5 OGL rules.

Many players and Gamemasters would frequently find themselves forgetting about the benefits of Skill Synergy at key moments or finding it would slow down play by creating a need to double check the rules to remember when it could be used. Arguably, these issues were especially problematic for Gamemasters who frequently keep track of numerous Non-Player Characters (NPCs) and their skills. Fortunately for players and Gamemasters alike, this work addresses these problems by reintroducing Skill Synergy in a retooled, easily referenced fashion.

To employ Skill Synergy, *Superior Synergy: Fantasy PFRPG Edition* utilizes a new system of relationships between related skills whereby applying a **Synergy Effect** to a desired **Primary Skill** first requires the character make a skill check for the complimentary **Synergy Skill** that is supposed to confer the synergy benefit. On the accompanying table, compare the Synergy Skill's check result relative to the DC to determine what the Synergy Effect is.

A character wants to take advantage of the Do It or Else! Synergy Effect for a DC 17 Intimidate check. This means the character must first make a DC 15 (Primary Skill DC - 2) Bluff check. A 6 is rolled, which is 9 less than the DC required for success. Checking this Synergy Effect's results table, we look along the "DC -5 to -9" row to see what the ramifications will be for the Primary Skill check.

Another new aspect of the revised Skill Synergy system is adding negative repercussions for the Primary Skill if the Synergy Skill's check fails, adding an

Skill Synergy as a Matter of Class

Despite the new mechanics introduced in this product towards making Skill Synergy more balanced, some Gamemasters may still have some concerns. A simple way of restricting Skill Synergy somewhat is to rule that characters may only employ it for a Primary Skill that is counted among their class skills. This underscores the character's focus on a specific range of skills, making Skill Synergy a reflection of this emphasis.

element of risk to the Skill Synergy process. In game terms, this means that the peripheral information or ability one can draw upon to help with an intended skill use is not always certain. It is as open to mistakes as is any other skill check. Skill Synergy has the potential to be a great boon, but it can also mislead the character or otherwise cause them problems that can hamper the skill performance.

Terms of Skill Synergy

DC: This indicates the Synergy Skill's DC for conferring its Synergy Effect unto the Primary Skill. The DC is a modification of the Primary Skill's DC.

Action: The type of action required to invoke the Synergy Effect. A Synergy Effect that requires some degree of action on the part of the Synergy Skill means the action is usually the norm for the latter. If the Synergy Effect requires utilizing knowledge or the like that is inherent to the Synergy Skill, the action required for the Synergy Effect can vary to suit the degree of time needed to get one's thoughts in order, although no additional required action is the norm in such cases.

Primary Skill: The skill that is to receive the benefits of synergy with another skill.

Synergy Skill: The skill that is to influence the Primary Skill via the Synergy's Skill's Synergy Effect.

Synergy Effect: The desired benefit (or unintentional detriment) bestowed upon a Primary Skill by a Synergy Skill check.

2. Skill Synergy

Multiple Synergy Effects

In instances where a Primary Skill has more than one Synergy Skill listed, it is usually possible to attempt more than one Synergy Effect for a single Primary Skill. Doing so requires separately spending the required time for each Synergy Skill and making separate skill checks for them. Multiple free action Synergy Effects can occur simultaneously. If these checks are not made consecutively—meaning no time is taken between Synergy Skill checks to do something else, regardless of how long the respective Synergy Skill checks take—all previous Synergy Effects are lost.

All Synergy Skill DCs are cumulatively increased by +2 per previous Synergy Effect already influencing a Primary Skill. Failing on any Synergy Skill check has the additional consequence of cancelling any previously obtained Synergy Effects, even if the effect is related to a different Synergy Skill.

In a similar vein, you can also try re-rolling a previous Synergy Skill in an attempt to get a better result than was previously achieved, but doing so follows the rules for attempting Multiple Synergy Effects (that is to say, it suffers the DC +2 cumulative modifier and failure wipes out any previous successes.) If the replacement Synergy Skill check succeeds and obtains a better result, use its Synergy Effect instead of that of the previous check (do not combine them), but if the check succeeds but obtains a reduced benefit you are permitted to retain the previously obtained, more favorable Synergy Effect.

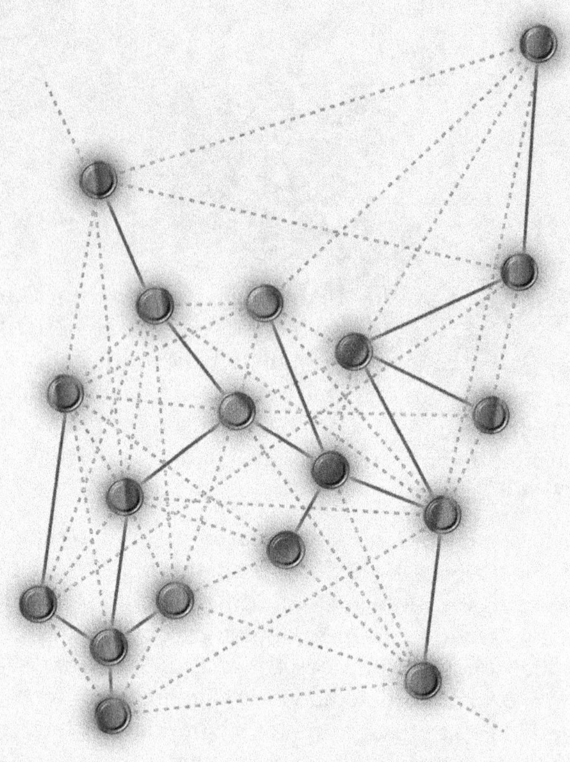

Skill Synergy Effects

Primary Skill	Synergy Skill	Synergy Effect
Appraise	Craft (various)	Assess Item
	Craft (various)	Reconsider Assessment
Bluff	Acrobatics	Twisting Feint
	Intimidate	Bluster
	Linguistics	Twisting Words
Climb	Acrobatics	Like a Monkey
Craft (alchemy)	Knowledge (nature)	Prime Ingredient
Craft (carpentry)	Knowledge (engineering)	Measure Twice, Cut Once
Craft (stonemasonry)	Knowledge (engineering)	Measure Twice, Chisel Once
Craft (traps)	Craft (carpentry)	Dangerous Woodcraft
	Craft (stonemasonry)	Perilous Stonework
	Stealth	Know How to Hide It
Diplomacy	Bluff	Silver Tongued
	Knowledge (various)	Travel in the Same Circles
	Sense Motive	Discern Meaning
Disable Device	Craft (locks)	Locksmith
	Craft (traps)	Trap Springer
	Craft (various)	Tear It Down
Disguise	Bluff	Sell the Story
	Perform (act)	Become the Role
Escape Artist	Acrobatics	Hard to Hold
	Sleight of Hand	Slip the Knot
Fly	Acrobatics	Aerobatics
Heal	Knowledge (nature)	Nature's Remedy
Intimidate	Bluff	Do It or Else!
	Bluff	Fear Me!
Knowledge (nature)	Survival	Know the Wilds
Perception	Knowledge (engineering)	Locate the Hidden
	Sense Motive	Something's Not Right
Perform (comedy)	Acrobatics	Slapstick
Perform (dance)	Acrobatics	Surprise Moves
Profession (various)	Knowledge (various)	In the Know
Ride	Handle Animal	Know Your Mount
Sense Motive	Diplomacy	Spot the Tell
	Perception	Gut Feeling
	Perception	Wink, Wink, Say No More
	Spellcraft	See the Signs
Sleight of Hand	Bluff	Confident Facade
Spellcraft	Knowledge (arcana)	Lore of Mysteries
	Use Magic Device	Scroll Reader
Survival	Knowledge (dungeoneering)	Tunnel Rat
	Knowledge (geography)	Lay of the Land
	Knowledge (nature)	Wilderness Awareness
	Knowledge (planes)	Otherworldly Awareness
	Perception	Spot the Trail
Use Magic Device	Linguistics	Read Spell Scroll
	Spellcraft	Decrypt Scroll

The Skills

Here you will find a list of Primary Skills accompanies by relevant Synergy Skills and the information required for assessing the latter's ability to impart a Synergy Effect. Only skills that may benefit from Skill Synergy appear here.

Appraise

The following Synergy Skills may benefit the Appraise skill.

Craft (various)—Assess Item

Knowing how to create something makes appraising the value of similar objects much easier.

This Synergy Effect from Craft only applies to Appraise checks made regarding items related to the specific Craft skill being used as a Synergy Skill. Furthermore, the Craft skill must be appropriate for the item being appraised; Craft: Bow will not offer any benefit when using Appraise on jewelry, for example.

DC: Primary Skill DC - 5

Action: None

Craft—Assess Item

Check Result	Synergy Effect
DC -15 or lower	−4 to the Appraise check
DC -10 to -14	−3 to the Appraise check
DC -5 to -9	−2 to the Appraise check
DC -1 to -4	−1 to the Appraise check
DC +0 to +4	+1 to the Appraise check
DC +5 to +9	+2 to the Appraise check
DC +10 to +14	+3 to the Appraise check
DC +15 to +19	+4 to the Appraise check
DC +20 or more	+5 to the Appraise check

Craft (various)—Reconsider Assessment

Knowing how to create something allows you to rethink your previous appraisal of an item's value, an action you are not normally allowed.

This Synergy Effect from Craft only applies to Appraise checks made regarding items related to the specific Craft skill being used as a Synergy Skill. Furthermore, the Craft skill must be appropriate for the item being appraised; Craft (carpentry) will not afford the sort of expertise that will allow one to reconsider their assessment of a suit of armor, for example.

DC: Primary Skill DC + 5

Craft—Reconsider Assessment

Check Result	Synergy Effect
DC -15 or lower	You may try again on a previously failed Appraise check, but even if the Appraise check succeeds your estimate will be 50% off. Quadruple the original inaccurate estimate if the Appraise check fails.
DC -10 to -14	You may try again on a previously failed Appraise check, but even if the Appraise check succeeds your estimate will be 25% off. Quadruple the original inaccurate estimate if the Appraise check fails.
DC -5 to -9	You may try again on a previously failed Appraise check, but even if the Appraise check succeeds your estimate will be 15% off. Triple the original inaccurate estimate if the Appraise check fails.
DC -1 to -4	You may try again on a previously failed Appraise check, but even if the Appraise check succeeds your estimate will be 10% off. Double the original inaccurate estimate if the Appraise check fails.
DC +0 to +4	You may try again on a previously failed Appraise check, but the additional focus required to reconsider your previous assessment requires 4 full actions, or 2 minutes to determine the most valuable items in a treasure hoard.
DC +5 to +9	You may try again on a previously failed Appraise check, but the additional focus required to reconsider your previous assessment requires 2 full actions, or 1 minute to determine the most valuable items in a treasure hoard.
DC +10 to +14	You may try again on a previously failed Appraise check, but the additional focus required to reconsider your previous assessment requires 1 full action, or 5 full actions to determine the most valuable items in a treasure hoard.
DC +15 to +19	You may try again on a previously failed Appraise check. Doing so requires the usual amount of time for an Appraise check.
DC +20 or more	You may try again on a previously failed Appraise check. Doing so requires half the usual amount of time for an Appraise check.

Action: 1 standard action. You must, however, take at least a day between your initial assessment and the reconsideration in order to clear your thoughts regarding the object's craftsmanship. You need not study the object during this time.

> **Appraise as Primary Skill:** Craft
>
> **Appraise as Synergy Skill:** None

Bluff

The following Synergy Skills may benefit the Bluff skill.

Acrobatics—Twisting Feint

Limberness and acrobatic talent can be used alongside Bluff to increase the chances of feinting by twisting and turning the body in unusual ways, making one's opponent less likely to differentiate the true strike from the false one.

This Synergy Effect from Acrobatics only applies to Bluff checks made to feint, and not for lies or secret messages.

DC: Primary Skill DC + 7

Action: 1 free action

Acrobatics—Twisting Feint

Check Result	Synergy Effect
DC -15 or lower	−2 to the Bluff check and decrease the AC bonus of the feint by −2 (to a minimum of no AC benefit)
DC -10 to -14	−2 to the Bluff check and decrease the AC bonus of the feint by −1 (to a minimum of no AC benefit)
DC -5 to -9	−1 to the Bluff check and decrease the AC bonus of the feint by −1 (to a minimum of no AC benefit)
DC -1 to -4	−1 to the Bluff check
DC +0 to +4	+1 to the Bluff check
DC +5 to +9	+1 to the Bluff check and increase the AC bonus for the feint by +1
DC +10 to +14	+2 to the Bluff check and increase the AC bonus for the feint by +1
DC +15 to +19	+2 to the Bluff check and increase the AC bonus for the feint by +2
DC +20 or more	+3 to the Bluff check and increase the AC bonus for the feint by +2

Intimidate—Bluster

Someone skilled at intimidating others can use that ability to put a subject off balance while attempting a bluff.

This Synergy Effect from Intimidate only applies to Bluff checks made to lie, and not for feints or secret messages.

DC: Primary Skill DC + 5

Action: None; the intimidation occurs during the words leading up to the Bluff check.

Intimidate—Bluster

Check Result	Synergy Effect
DC -15 or lower	−4 to the Bluff check
DC -10 to -14	−3 to the Bluff check
DC -5 to -9	−2 to the Bluff check
DC -1 to -4	−1 to the Bluff check
DC +0 to +4	+1 to the Bluff check
DC +5 to +9	+2 to the Bluff check
DC +10 to +14	+3 to the Bluff check
DC +15 to +19	+4 to the Bluff check
DC +20 or more	+5 to the Bluff check

Linguistics—Twisting Words

A skilled linguist, using his superior understanding of a language, may better hide hidden meaning in what he says.

This Synergy Effect from Linguistics only applies to Bluff checks made to convey secret messages, and not to lie or feint.

DC: Primary Skill DC + 5

Action: None; the secret message is imparted within the words leading up to the Bluff check.

> **Bluff as Primary Skill:** Acrobatics, Intimidate, Linguistics
>
> **Bluff as Synergy Skill:** Diplomacy, Disguise, Intimidate, Sleight of Hand

Linguistics—Twisting Words

Check Result	Synergy Effect
DC -15 or lower	−2 to the Bluff check; failing the bluff means the wrong message will be very detrimental, such as subject failing to show up at the correct location for a dangerous meeting where the subject was meant to act as backup.
DC -10 to -14	−2 to the Bluff check; failing the bluff means the wrong message will be somewhat detrimentat, such as causing the subject to wear something inappropriate to an appointment.
DC -5 to -9	−1 to the Bluff check; failing the bluff means the wrong message will be somewhat detrimental, such as causing the subject to wear something inappropriate to an appointment.
DC -1 to -4	−1 to the Bluff check
DC +0 to +4	+1 to the Bluff check
DC +5 to +9	+2 to the Bluff check and unintended recipients suffer a -1 Sense Motive penalty to decipher the secret message
DC +10 to +14	+3 to the Bluff check and unintended recipients suffer a -1 Sense Motive penalty to decipher the secret message
DC +15 to +19	+4 to the Bluff check and unintended recipients suffer a -2 Sense Motive penalty to decipher the secret message
DC +20 or more	+5 to the Bluff check and unintended recipients suffer a -2 Sense Motive penalty to decipher the secret message

Climb

The following Synergy Skill may benefit the Climb skill.

Acrobatics—Like a Monkey

Your nimbleness and sense of balance allows you to twist, spin, and teeter in ways that increase your chances of grabbing something or someone that is falling, or to grab onto something if you are yourself falling.

This Synergy Effect from Acrobatics only applies to Climb checks to catch yourself or someone else while climbing.

DC: Primary Skill DC - 5

Action: 1 free action

> **Climb as Primary Skill:** Acrobatics
>
> **Climb as Synergy Skill:** None

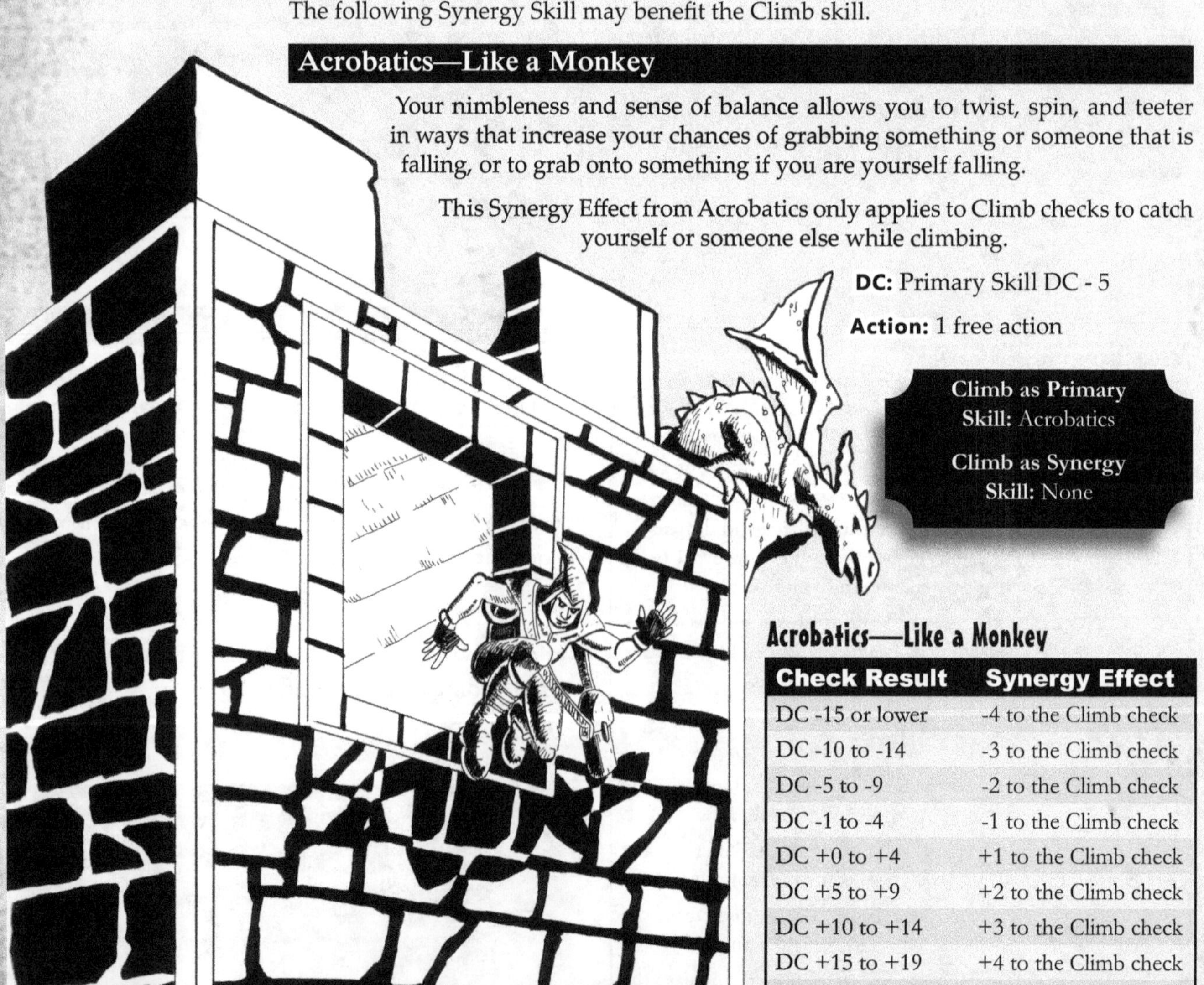

Acrobatics—Like a Monkey

Check Result	Synergy Effect
DC -15 or lower	-4 to the Climb check
DC -10 to -14	-3 to the Climb check
DC -5 to -9	-2 to the Climb check
DC -1 to -4	-1 to the Climb check
DC +0 to +4	+1 to the Climb check
DC +5 to +9	+2 to the Climb check
DC +10 to +14	+3 to the Climb check
DC +15 to +19	+4 to the Climb check
DC +20 or more	+5 to the Climb check

Craft (alchemy)

The following Synergy Skill may benefit the Craft (alchemy) skill.

Knowledge (nature)—Prime Ingredient

A solid understanding of plants and other aspects of nature from which alchemical ingredients may be derived may allow the creation of certain alchemical items with greater ease.

This Synergy Effect from Knowledge (nature) only applies to Craft (alchemy) checks to create or repair alchemical items that require ingredients found in nature.

DC: Primary Skill DC + 3

Action: None

Knowledge (nature)—Prime Ingredient

Check Result	Synergy Effect
DC -15 or lower	-4 to the Craft (alchemy) check and if you fail the Craft check by 5 or more you ruin all of the raw materials
DC -10 to -14	-3 to the Craft (alchemy) check and if you fail the Craft check by 5 or more you ruin three-quarters of the raw materials
DC -5 to -9	-2 to the Craft (alchemy) check
DC -1 to -4	-1 to the Craft (alchemy) check
DC +0 to +4	+1 to the Craft (alchemy) check
DC +5 to +9	+2 to the Craft (alchemy) check
DC +10 to +14	+3 to the Craft (alchemy) check and if you fail the Craft check by 5 or more you only ruin one-third of the raw materials
DC +15 to +19	+4 to the Craft (alchemy) check and if you fail the Craft check by 5 or more you only ruin one-quarter of the raw materials
DC +20 or more	+5 to the Craft (alchemy) check and if you fail the Craft check by 5 or more you do not ruin any of the raw materials

Craft (alchemy) as Primary Skill:
Knowledge (nature)

Craft (alchemy) as Synergy Skill:
Appraise, Disable Device

Craft (carpentry)

The following Synergy Skill may benefit the Craft (carpentry) skill.

Knowledge (engineering)—Measure Twice, Cut Once

Training in engineering grants an understanding of load bearing, counter-balancing, and the like. This information compliments a carpenter's ability to erect a structure of wood.

This Synergy Effect from Knowledge (engineering) only applies to Craft (carpentry) checks to create or repair structures wholly or predominantly made of wood.

DC: Primary Skill DC - 5

Action: None

Knowledge (engineering)—Measure Twice, Cut Once

Check Result	Synergy Effect
DC -15 or lower	-4 to the Craft (carpentry) check and if you fail the Craft check by 5 or more you ruin all of the raw materials
DC -10 to -14	-3 to the Craft (carpentry) check and if you fail the Craft check by 5 or more you ruin three-quarters of the raw materials
DC -5 to -9	-2 to the Craft (carpentry) check
DC -1 to -4	-1 to the Craft (carpentry) check
DC +0 to +4	+1 to the Craft (carpentry) check
DC +5 to +9	+2 to the Craft (carpentry) check
DC +10 to +14	+3 to the Craft (carpentry) check and if you fail the Craft check by 5 or more you only ruin one-third of the raw materials
DC +15 to +19	+4 to the Craft (carpentry) check and if you fail the Craft check by 5 or more you only ruin one-quarter of the raw materials
DC +20 or more	+5 to the Craft (carpentry) check and if you fail the Craft check by 5 or more you do not ruin any of the raw materials

Craft (carpentry) as Primary Skill:
Knowledge (engineering)

Craft (carpentry) as Synergy Skill:
Appraise, Craft (traps), Disable Device

Craft (stonemasonry)

The following Synergy Skill may benefit the Craft (stonemasonry) skill.

Knowledge (engineering)— Measure Twice, Chisel Once

Engineer training permits a stonemason to better comprehend common principles of load bearing, counter-balancing, and other general aspects of erecting a structure. It also imparts additional awareness of concepts unique to stonework, such as the proper construction of a strong arc or dome.

This Synergy Effect from Knowledge (engineering) only applies to Craft (stonemasonry) checks to create or repair structures wholly or predominantly made of stone.

DC: Primary Skill DC - 5

Action: 1 free action

Knowledge (engineering)—Measure Twice, Chisel Once

Check Result	Synergy Effect
DC -15 or lower	-4 to the Craft (stonemasonry) check and if you fail the Craft check by 5 or more you ruin all of the raw materials
DC -10 to -14	-3 to the Craft (stonemasonry) check and if you fail the Craft check by 5 or more you ruin three-quarters of the raw materials
DC -5 to -9	-2 to the Craft (stonemasonry) check
DC -1 to -4	-1 to the Craft (stonemasonry) check
DC +0 to +4	+1 to the Craft (stonemasonry) check
DC +5 to +9	+1 to the Craft (stonemasonry) check and the structure has 20 hp/in. of thickness if the Craft check succeeds
DC +10 to +14	+2 to the Craft (stonemasonry) check and the structure has 20 hp/in. of thickness if the Craft check succeeds
DC +15 to +19	+2 to the Craft (stonemasonry) check and the structure has 25 hp/in. of thickness if the Craft check succeeds
DC +20 or more	+3 to the Craft (stonemasonry) check and the structure has 25 hp/in. of thickness if the Craft check succeeds

Craft (stonemasonry) as Primary Skill: Knowledge (engineering)

Craft (stonemasonry) as Synergy Skill: Appraise, Craft (traps), Disable Device

Craft (traps)

The following Synergy Skills may benefit the Craft (traps) skill.

Craft (carpentry)—Dangerous Woodcraft

The better one is at working with wood, the better the traps one may make primarily or entirely out of this material. This is because of a better understanding of how the material can perform within the intended design.

This Synergy Effect from Craft (carpentry) only applies to Craft (trap) checks to create or repair traps made entirely or mostly out of wood.

DC: Primary Skill DC + 5

Action: None

Craft (carpentry)—Dangerous Woodcraft

Check Result	Synergy Effect
DC -15 or lower	-4 to the Craft (carpentry) check and increase any associated costs by 50%
DC -10 to -14	-3 to the Craft (carpentry) check and increase any associated costs by 25%
DC -5 to -9	-2 to the Craft (carpentry) check and increase any associated costs by 10%
DC -1 to -4	-1 to the Craft (carpentry) check
DC +0 to +4	+1 to the Craft (carpentry) check
DC +5 to +9	+2 to the Craft (carpentry) check and reduce any associated costs by 10%
DC +10 to +14	+3 to the Craft (carpentry) check and reduce any associated costs by 10%
DC +15 to +19	+4 to the Craft (carpentry) check and reduce any associated costs by 25%
DC +20 or more	+5 to the Craft (carpentry) check and reduce any associated costs by 25%

Craft (stonemasonry)—Perilous Stonework

The better one is at working with stone, the better the traps one may make primarily or entirely out stone. This is because of a better understanding of how the material can perform within the intended design.

This Synergy Effect from Craft (stonemasonry) only applies to Craft (trap) checks to create or repair traps made entirely or mostly out of stone.

DC: Primary Skill DC

Action: None

Craft (stonemasonry)—Perilous Stonework

Check Result	Synergy Effect
DC -15 or lower	-4 to the Craft (stonemasonry) check and double any associated costs
DC -10 to -14	-3 to the Craft (stonemasonry) check and increase any associated costs by 50%
DC -5 to -9	-2 to the Craft (stonemasonry) check and increase any associated costs by 25%
DC -1 to -4	-1 to the Craft (stonemasonry) check
DC +0 to +4	+1 to the Craft (stonemasonry) check
DC +5 to +9	+2 to the Craft (stonemasonry) check and reduce any associated costs by 10%
DC +10 to +14	+3 to the Craft (stonemasonry) check and reduce any associated costs by 10%
DC +15 to +19	+4 to the Craft (stonemasonry) check and reduce any associated costs by 25%
DC +20 or more	+5 to the Craft (stonemasonry) check and reduce any associated costs by 25%

Stealth—Know How to Hide It

Someone who is skilled at hiding themselves can use that knowledge to better conceal a trap.

This Synergy Effect from Stealth only applies to Craft (traps) checks to create a trap requiring a DC 20 or higher Perception check to notice.

DC: Primary Skill DC + 5

Action: None

Stealth—Know How to Hide It

Check Result	Synergy Effect
DC -15 or lower	Even if the Craft (traps) check is successful, reduce the trap's Perception DC by -5, although the trap's DC for the purpose of creation and repair remains unchanged by this
DC -10 to -14	Even if the Craft (traps) check is successful, reduce the trap's Perception DC by -2, although the trap's DC for the purpose of creation and repair remains unchanged by this
DC -5 to -9	Even if the Craft (traps) check is successful, reduce the trap's Perception DC by -1, although the trap's DC for the purpose of creation and repair remains unchanged by this
DC -1 to -4	Even if the Craft (traps) check is successful, reduce the trap's Perception DC by -1, although the trap's DC for the purpose of creation and repair remains unchanged by this
DC +0 to +4	A successful Craft (traps) check will increase the trap's Perception DC by +1 without affecting the DC to create or repair the trap
DC +5 to +9	A successful Craft (traps) check will increase the trap's Perception DC by +2 without affecting the DC to create or repair the trap
DC +10 to +14	A successful Craft (traps) check will increase the trap's Perception DC by +5 without affecting the DC to create or repair the trap
DC +15 to +19	A successful Craft (traps) check will increase the trap's Perception DC by +10 without affecting the DC to create or repair the trap
DC +20 or more	A successful Craft (traps) check will increase the trap's Perception DC by +15 without affecting the DC to create or repair the trap

Craft (traps) as Primary Skill:
Craft (carpentry), Craft (stonemasonry), Stealth

Craft (traps) as Synergy Skill:
Appraise, Disable Device

Diplomacy

The following Synergy Skills may benefit the Diplomacy skill.

Bluff—Silver Tongued

Someone who is good at bluffing has a better chance of convincing the subject of their diplomacy that they have more strength behind their position than is true.

This Synergy Effect from Bluff only applies to Diplomacy checks made to change an NPC's attitude or make a request of a NPC.

DC: Primary Skill DC

Action: None; the act of bluffing occurs during the words leading up to the Diplomacy check.

Bluff—Silver Tongued

Check Result	Synergy Effect
DC -15 or lower	*Improve attitude*: −3 to the Diplomacy check and failing the Diplomacy check decreases the attitude to Hostile; *Make a request*: -4 to the Diplomacy check
DC -10 to -14	*Improve attitude*: −2 to the Diplomacy check and failing the Diplomacy check decreases the attitude by three steps; *Make a request*: -3 to the Diplomacy check
DC -5 to -9	*Improve attitude*: −1 to the Diplomacy check and failing the Diplomacy check decreases the attitude by two steps; *Make a request*: -2 to the Diplomacy check
DC -1 to -4	−1 to the Diplomacy check
DC +0 to +4	+1 to the Diplomacy check
DC +5 to +9	(d20, 1 to 10) +2 to the Diplomacy check *or* (11 to 20) the Diplomacy check takes half the usual time
DC +10 to +14	+2 to the Diplomacy check and the Diplomacy check takes half the usual time
DC +15 to +19	(d20, 1 to 10) +3 to the Diplomacy check *or* (11 to 20) the Diplomacy check takes one-quarter the usual time (minimum of 1 move action)
DC +20 or more	+3 to the Diplomacy check and the Diplomacy check takes one-quarter the usual time (minimum of 1 move action)

Knowledge (various)—Travel in the Same Circles

Some fields of Knowledge and can provide diplomatic leverage, such as may be achieved by creating a tactful bridge based on shared understanding or experiences. Gamemasters must decide when a Knowledge skill may provide such a Synergy Effect., but such instances are most common among fields of Knowledge rooted in culture, such as Knowledge (nobility) or Knowledge (religion.)

This Synergy Effect from Knowledge applies to Diplomacy checks the Gamemaster feels are appropriate to the circumstances. For example, a Gamemaster may decide Knowledge (local) is helpful with a *gather information* check but has no role to play with improving a NPC's attitude.

DC: Primary Skill DC + 3

Action: None

Knowledge (various)—Travel in the Same Circles

Check Result	Synergy Effect
DC -15 or lower	-4 to the Diplomacy check
DC -10 to -14	-3 to the Diplomacy check
DC -5 to -9	-2 to the Diplomacy check
DC -1 to -4	-1 to the Diplomacy check
DC +0 to +4	+1 to the Diplomacy check
DC +5 to +9	+2 to the Diplomacy check
DC +10 to +14	+3 to the Diplomacy check
DC +15 to +19	+4 to the Diplomacy check
DC +20 or more	+5 to the Diplomacy check

Sense Motive—Discern Meaning

Carefully studying one's opponent can provide an edge during acts of diplomacy.

This Synergy Effect from Sense Motive applies to all Diplomacy checks.

DC: Primary Skill DC

Action: Double the amount of time required of the Diplomacy action

Sense Motive—Discern Meaning

Check Result	Synergy Effect
DC -15 or lower	-4 to the Diplomacy check
DC -10 to -14	-3 to the Diplomacy check
DC -5 to -9	-2 to the Diplomacy check
DC -1 to -4	-1 to the Diplomacy check
DC +0 to +4	+1 to the Diplomacy check
DC +5 to +9	+2 to the Diplomacy check
DC +10 to +14	+3 to the Diplomacy check
DC +15 to +19	+4 to the Diplomacy check
DC +20 or more	+5 to the Diplomacy check

Diplomacy as Primary Skill:
Bluff, Knowledge, Sense Motive

Diplomacy as Synergy Skill: Sense Motive

Disable Device

The following Synergy Skills may benefit the Disable Device skill.

Craft (locks)—Locksmith

Someone who is skilled at creating and repairing locks is more likely to know the tricks to open them while locked and no key is at hand.

This Synergy Effect from Craft (locks) only applies to Disable Device checks to open locks.

DC: Primary Skill DC - 5

Action: Double the Disable Device check's action

Craft (locks)—Locksmith

Check Result	Synergy Effect
DC -15 or lower	-4 to the Disable Device check and a -3 penalty is applied to Perception checks to notice any traps on the lock
DC -10 to -14	-3 to the Disable Device check and a -2 penalty is applied to Perception checks to notice any traps on the lock
DC -5 to -9	-2 to the Disable Device check and a -1 penalty is applied to Perception checks to notice any traps on the lock
DC -1 to -4	-1 to the Disable Device check
DC +0 to +4	+1 to the Disable Device check
DC +5 to +9	+2 to the Disable Device check
DC +10 to +14	+3 to the Disable Device check and the Gamemaster makes a secret Perception check to see if you inadvertently notice any traps on the lock
DC +15 to +19	+4 to the Disable Device check and the Gamemaster makes a secret Perception check at +1 to see if you inadvertently notice any traps on the lock
DC +20 or more	+5 to the Disable Device check and the Gamemaster makes a secret Perception check at +2 to see if you inadvertently notice any traps on the lock

Craft (traps)—Trap Springer

Understanding how traps are built makes someone encountering a trap more aware of triggering mechanisms, deployment methods, and techniques for disabling or circumventing such devices.

This Synergy Effect from Craft (traps) only applies to Disable Device checks to disarm or bypass a trap.

DC: Primary Skill DC + 5

Action: Double the Disable Device check's action

Craft (traps)—Trap Springer

Check Result	Synergy Effect
DC -15 or lower	-4 to the Disable Device check and even if the check is successful the trap cannot be bypassed without being disarmed
DC -10 to -14	-3 to the Disable Device check and even if the check is successful the roll needs to beat the trap's DC by 15 or more in order to bypass it without disarming it
DC -5 to -9	-2 to the Disable Device check and even if the check is successful the roll needs to beat the trap's DC by 13 or more in order to bypass it without disarming it
DC -1 to -4	-1 to the Disable Device check
DC +0 to +4	+1 to the Disable Device check
DC +5 to +9	+2 to the Disable Device check
DC +10 to +14	+3 to the Disable Device check and the roll need only beat the trap's DC by 7 or more in order to bypass it without disarming it
DC +15 to +19	+4 to the Disable Device check and the roll need only beat the trap's DC by 5 or more in order to bypass it without disarming it
DC +20 or more	+5 to the Disable Device check and if the check is successful the trap can be bypassed without being disarmed

Craft (various)—Tear It Down

If you know how to build something you have a better perspective on how to destroy it, even if it has been built by someone else.

This Synergy Effect from Craft only applies to Disable Device checks to sabotage mechanical devices that can be created or repaired using the specified Craft skill.

DC: Primary Skill DC - 5

Action: 1 full-round action

2. SKILL SYNERGY

Craft—Tear It Down

Check Result	Synergy Effect
DC -15 or lower	-4 to the Disable Device check and increase the time required by 2d4 rounds
DC -10 to -14	-3 to the Disable Device check and increase the time required by 1d4 rounds
DC -5 to -9	-2 to the Disable Device check and increase the time required by 1 round
DC -1 to -4	-1 to the Disable Device check
DC +0 to +4	+1 to the Disable Device check
DC +5 to +9	+1 to the Disable Device check and reduce the time required by 1 round (minimum 1 round)
DC +10 to +14	+2 to the Disable Device check and reduce the time required by 1 round (minimum 1 round)
DC +15 to +19	+2 to the Disable Device check and reduce the time required by 2d4 rounds (minimum 1 round)
DC +20 or more	+3 to the Disable Device check and reduce the time required by 2d4 rounds (minimum 1 round)

Disable Device as Primary Skill:
Craft (locks), Craft (traps), Craft (various)

Disable Device as Synergy Skill: None

Disguise

The following Synergy Skills may benefit the Disguise skill.

Bluff—Sell the Story

If in disguise and being observed, a good lie or exaggeration can certainly help you act in character or explain any discrepancies, even if the observer has reason to be suspicious of you.

This Synergy Effect from Bluff can be attempted each time a Perception check is made to oppose the Disguise check, modifying the latter's original result accordingly for that check alone.

DC: Primary Skill DC

Action: 1 full-round action or longer, depending upon how long the Gamemaster feels is required to make the Bluff

Bluff—Sell the Story

Check Result	Synergy Effect
DC -15 or lower	-4 to the Disguise check
DC -10 to -14	-3 to the Disguise check
DC -5 to -9	-2 to the Disguise check
DC -1 to -4	-1 to the Disguise check
DC +0 to +4	+1 to the Disguise check
DC +5 to +9	+2 to the Disguise check
DC +10 to +14	+3 to the Disguise check
DC +15 to +19	+4 to the Disguise check
DC +20 or more	+5 to the Disguise check

Perform (act)—Become the Role

An actor is able to compliment the visual disguise with appropriate behavior, changes of voice, and similar techniques that make what others see more believable.

This Synergy Effect from Perform (act) can be made each time a Perception check is made to oppose the Disguise check, modifying the latter's original result accordingly for that check alone.

DC: Primary Skill DC

Action: 1 full-round action or longer, depending upon how long the Gamemaster feels is required to properly act the part

Disguise as Primary Skill: Bluff, Perform (act)

Disguise as Synergy Skill: None

Escape Artist

The following Synergy Skills may benefit the Escape Artist skill.

Acrobatics—Hard to Hold

The ability to flip and twist one's body comes in handy when the time comes to squeeze out of a binding grip.

This Synergy Effect from Acrobatics only applies to Escape Artist checks to escape a grapple.

DC: Primary Skill DC + 5

Action: 1 free action

Perform (act)—Become the Role

Check Result	Synergy Effect
DC -15 or lower	-2 to the Disguise check and if impersonating someone specific, Perception checks to see through the disguise are made upon meeting you and every fifteen minutes of exposure thereafter
DC -10 to -14	-2 to the Disguise check and if impersonating someone specific, Perception checks to see through the disguise are made upon meeting you and every half hour of exposure thereafter
DC -5 to -9	-1 to the Disguise check and if impersonating someone specific, Perception checks to see through the disguise are made upon meeting you and every half hour of exposure thereafter
DC -1 to -4	-1 to the Disguise check
DC +0 to +4	+1 to the Disguise check
DC +5 to +9	+1 to the Disguise check and if impersonating someone specific, Perception checks to see through the disguise are made upon meeting you and every two hours of exposure thereafter
DC +10 to +14	+2 to the Disguise check and if impersonating someone specific, Perception checks to see through the disguise are made upon meeting you and every two hours of exposure thereafter
DC +15 to +19	+2 to the Disguise check and if impersonating someone specific, Perception checks to see through the disguise are made upon meeting you and every three hours of exposure thereafter
DC +20 or more	+3 to the Disguise check and if impersonating someone specific, Perception checks to see through the disguise are made upon meeting you and every three hours of exposure thereafter

Acrobatics—Hard to Hold

Check Result	Synergy Effect
DC -15 or lower	-4 to the Escape Artist check but if you fail to escape the grapple your opponent can immediately move, damage, or pin you as a free action, even if their turn would normally be done for the round
DC -10 to -14	-3 to the Escape Artist check
DC -5 to -9	-2 to the Escape Artist check
DC -1 to -4	-1 to the Escape Artist check
DC +0 to +4	+1 to the Escape Artist check
DC +5 to +9	+2 to the Escape Artist check
DC +10 to +14	+3 to the Escape Artist check
DC +15 to +19	+4 to the Escape Artist check
DC +20 or more	+5 to the Escape Artist check and if you reverse the grapple you can choose to immediately move, damage, or pin your opponent as a free action

Sleight of Hand—Slip the Knot

Check Result	Synergy Effect
DC -15 or lower	-4 to the Escape Artist check and escaping requires triple the usual time
DC -10 to -14	-3 to the Escape Artist check and escaping requires double the usual time
DC -5 to -9	-2 to the Escape Artist check and escaping requires 50% more time
DC -1 to -4	-1 to the Escape Artist check
DC +0 to +4	+1 to the Escape Artist check
DC +5 to +9	+2 to the Escape Artist check and escaping only requires half the usual time (minimum of 1 move action)
DC +10 to +14	+3 to the Escape Artist check and escaping only requires half the usual time (minimum of 1 move action)
DC +15 to +19	+4 to the Escape Artist check and escaping only requires one-quarter the usual time (minimum of 1 move action)
DC +20 or more	+5 to the Escape Artist check and escaping only requires one-quarter the usual time (minimum of 1 move action)

Sleight of Hand—Slip the Knot

You can maneuver and contort your hands in order to more easily slip bindings.

This Synergy Effect from Sleight of Hand only applies to Escape Artist checks to escape ropes or escape manacles or masterwork manacles.

DC: Primary Skill DC + 5

Action: 1 free action

Escape Artist as Primary Skill: Acrobatics, Sleight of Hand

Escape Artist as Synergy Skill: None

2. Skill Synergy

Fly

The following Synergy Skill may benefit the Fly skill.

Acrobatics—Aerobatics

The improved sense of balance and increased flexibility that comes with Acrobatics can make many maneuvers and recovery actions while flying easier.

This Synergy Effect from Acrobatics only applies to Fly checks made to turn greater than 45° by spending 5 feet of movement, turn 180° by spending 10 feet of movement, fly up at greater than 45° angle, for a collision while flying, to avoid falling damage, or for any other complex maneuver the Gamemaster rules is appropriate.

DC: Primary Skill DC + 5

Action: 1 free action

Fly as Primary Skill: Acrobatics

Fly as Synergy Skill: None

Acrobatics—Aerobatics

Check Result	Synergy Effect
DC -15 or lower	-4 to the Fly check and, if it is normally required, 15 feet of additional movement is spent on the maneuver
DC -10 to -14	-3 to the Fly check and, if it is normally required, 10 feet of additional movement is spent on the maneuver
DC -5 to -9	-2 to the Fly check and, if it is normally required, 5 feet of additional movement is spent on the maneuver
DC -1 to -4	-1 to the Fly check
DC +0 to +4	+1 to the Fly check
DC +5 to +9	+2 to the Fly check
DC +10 to +14	+3 to the Fly check
DC +15 to +19	+4 to the Fly check and, if it is normally required, 5 feet less of additional movement is spent on the maneuver (to a minimum of 5 additional feet)
DC +20 or more	+5 to the Fly check and, if it is normally required, no additional movement is spent on the maneuver

Heal

The following Synergy Skill may benefit the Heal skill.

Knowledge (nature)—Nature's Remedy

Knowing how to use what nature has provided in a way that may improve healing.

This Synergy Effect from Knowledge (nature) only applies to Heal checks involving treatments using natural ingredients. Not everything in nature is helpful with healing, however, so Gamemasters will need to use their judgment as to when this is allowed.

Knowledge (nature)—Nature's Remedy

Check Result	Synergy Effect
DC -15 or lower	-4 to the Heal check and providing first aid, treat wounds from caltrops, or treat poison requires one minute; treat disease or tend wound for *spike growth* or *spike stones* takes 20 minutes; treat deadly wounds takes 2 hours; long-term care requires 16 hours
DC -10 to -14	-3 to the Heal check and providing first aid, treat wounds from caltrops, or treat poison is a full-round action; treat disease or tend wound for *spike growth* or *spike stones* takes 15 minutes; treat deadly wounds takes 1 and a half hours; long-term care requires 12 hours
DC -5 to -9	-2 to the Heal check
DC -1 to -4	-1 to the Heal check
DC +0 to +4	+1 to the Heal check
DC +5 to +9	+2 to the Heal check
DC +10 to +14	+3 to the Heal check and treat disease or tend wound for *spike growth* or *spike stones* takes 7 and a half minutes; treat deadly wounds takes 45 minutes; long-term care requires 6 hours
DC +15 to +19	+4 to the Heal check and treat disease or tend wound for *spike growth* or *spike stones* takes 5 minutes; treat deadly wounds takes 30 minutes; long-term care requires 4 hours
DC +20 or more	+5 to the Heal check and providing first aid, treat wounds from caltrops, or treat poison is a move action; treat disease or tend wound for *spike growth* or *spike stones* takes 2 and a half minutes (25 rounds); treat deadly wounds takes 15 minutes; long-term care requires 2 hours

DC: Primary Skill DC + 5

Action: 1 free action, plus whatever time is needed to gather the ingredients

> **Heal as Primary Skill:** Knowledge (nature)
>
> **Heal as Synergy Skill:** None

Intimidate

The following Synergy Skills may benefit the Intimidate skill.

Bluff—Do It or Else!

A good liar can make an attempt to frighten a subject into doing what one wants so long as it is convincing.

This Synergy Effect from Bluff only applies to Intimidate checks to make an opponent friendly towards you.

DC: Primary Skill DC - 2

Action: None; the act of bluffing occurs during the words leading up to the Intimidate check

Bluff—Do It or Else!

Check Result	Synergy Effect
DC -15 or lower	-2 to the Intimidate check but success means the opponent will only be friendly for 2d10 minutes
DC -10 to -14	-2 to the Intimidate check but success means the opponent will only be friendly for 1d4x10 minutes
DC -5 to -9	-1 to the Intimidate check but success means the opponent will only be friendly for 1d4x10 minutes
DC -1 to -4	-1 to the Intimidate check
DC +0 to +4	+1 to the Intimidate check
DC +5 to +9	+1 to the Intimidate check and success means the opponent will be friendly for 2d4x10 minutes
DC +10 to +14	+2 to the Intimidate check and success means the opponent will be friendly for 2d4x10 minutes
DC +15 to +19	+2 to the Intimidate check and success means the opponent will be friendly for 2d6x10 minutes
DC +20 or more	+3 to the Intimidate check and success means the opponent will be friendly for 2d6x10 minutes

2. Skill Synergy

Bluff—Fear Me!

A good bluff can convince an opponent that one poses a greater threat or is capable of greater violence than is actually the case, making it easier to shatter their nerve.

This Synergy Effect from Bluff only applies to Intimidate checks to demoralize an opponent.

DC: Primary Skill DC

Action: The Intimidate check now requires 1 full-round action

Bluff—Fear Me!

Check Result	Synergy Effect
DC -15 or lower	-2 to the Intimidate check and the opponent must be within 10 feet to be demoralized
DC -10 to -14	-2 to the Intimidate check and the opponent must be within 20 feet to be demoralized
DC -5 to -9	-1 to the Intimidate check and the opponent must be within 20 feet to be demoralized
DC -1 to -4	-1 to the Intimidate check
DC +0 to +4	+1 to the Intimidate check
DC +5 to +9	+1 to the Intimidate check and success means the opponent is demoralized for an additional round
DC +10 to +14	+2 to the Intimidate check and success means the opponent is demoralized for an additional round
DC +15 to +19	+2 to the Intimidate check and success means the opponent is demoralized for an additional 2 rounds
DC +20 or more	+3 to the Intimidate check and success means the opponent is demoralized for an additional 2 rounds

> **Intimidate as Primary Skill:** Bluff
>
> **Intimidate as Synergy Skill:** Bluff

Knowledge (nature)

The following Synergy Skill may benefit the Knowledge (nature) skill.

Survival—Know the Wilds

Someone trained to survive in the wilds can translate that experience and information into a more refined understanding of nature.

DC: Primary Skill DC + 5

Action: 1 free action

Survival—Know the Wilds

Check Result	Synergy Effect
DC -15 or lower	-4 to the Knowledge (nature) check
DC -10 to -14	-3 to the Knowledge (nature) check
DC -5 to -9	-2 to the Knowledge (nature) check
DC -1 to -4	-1 to the Knowledge (nature) check
DC +0 to +4	+1 to the Knowledge (nature) check
DC +5 to +9	+2 to the Knowledge (nature) check
DC +10 to +14	+3 to the Knowledge (nature) check
DC +15 to +19	+4 to the Knowledge (nature) check
DC +20 or more	+5 to the Knowledge (nature) check

> **Knowledge (nature) as Primary Skill:** Survival
>
> **Knowledge (nature) as Synergy Skill:** Craft (alchemy), Diplomacy, Heal, Profession (various), Survival

Perception

The following Synergy Skills may benefit the Perception skill.

Knowledge (engineering)— Locate the Hidden

Someone who understands the principles of engineering is perhaps better able than others to know what to look for when searching for secret doors, compartments, and the like.

This Synergy Effect from Knowledge (engineering) only applies to Perception checks to conduct an intentional search in a structure or something else that could benefit from engineering knowledge. Searching someone for something hidden on their person, for example, would not benefit from this Synergy Skill.

DC: Primary Skill DC

Action: 1 free action

Knowledge (engineering)—Locate the Hidden

Check Result	Synergy Effect
DC -15 or lower	-4 to the Perception check and an intentional search requires 1d4+1 rounds
DC -10 to -14	-3 to the Perception check and an intentional search is a full-round action
DC -5 to -9	-2 to the Perception check and an intentional search is a standard action
DC -1 to -4	-1 to the Perception check
DC +0 to +4	+1 to the Perception check
DC +5 to +9	+2 to the Perception check
DC +10 to +14	+3 to the Perception check and an intentional search is a swift action
DC +15 to +19	+4 to the Perception check and an intentional search is a swift action
DC +20 or more	+5 to the Perception check and an intentional search is a free action

Sense Motive—Something's Not Right

Being able to pick up on subtle hints in the subject's body language, words, and behavior can help the observer see through a disguise.

This Synergy Effect from Sense Motive only applies to Perception checks versus someone else's Disguise check.

DC: Primary Skill DC + 5

Action: 1 free action

Sense Motive—Something's Not Right

Check Result	Synergy Effect
DC -15 or lower	-2 to the Perception check and checks to see through the disguise are made upon meeting the subject and every three hours of exposure thereafter
DC -10 to -14	-2 to the Perception check and checks to see through the disguise are made upon meeting the subject and every two hours of exposure thereafter
DC -5 to -9	-1 to the Perception check and checks to see through the disguise are made upon meeting the subject and every two hours of exposure thereafter
DC -1 to -4	-1 to the Perception check
DC +0 to +4	+1 to the Perception check
DC +5 to +9	+1 to the Perception check and checks to see through the disguise are made upon meeting the subject and every half hour of exposure thereafter
DC +10 to +14	+2 to the Perception check and checks to see through the disguise are made upon meeting the subject and every half hour of exposure thereafter
DC +15 to +19	+2 to the Perception check and checks to see through the disguise are made upon meeting the subject and every fifteen minutes of exposure thereafter
DC +20 or more	+3 to the Perception check and checks to see through the disguise are made upon meeting the subject and every fifteen minutes of exposure thereafter

Perception as Primary Skill:
Knowledge (engineering), Sense Motive

Perception as Synergy Skill: Sense Motive

Perform: (comedy)

The following Synergy Skill may benefit the Perform (comedy) skill.

Acrobatics—Slapstick

Some forms of physical comedy, such as a jester's antics, can benefit from someone who can bend their body in unusual ways, jump great distances, or roll and spin about deftly.

This Synergy Effect from Acrobatics only applies to Perform (comedy) checks involving extreme physical comedy, such as dives, falls, and tumbling.

DC: Primary Skill DC + 5

Action: None; the acrobatics are integrated into the performance

Acrobatics—Slapstick

Check Result	Synergy Effect
DC -15 or lower	-4 to the Perform (comedy) check
DC -10 to -14	-3 to the Perform (comedy) check
DC -5 to -9	-2 to the Perform (comedy) check
DC -1 to -4	-1 to the Perform (comedy) check
DC +0 to +4	+1 to the Perform (comedy) check
DC +5 to +9	+2 to the Perform (comedy) check
DC +10 to +14	+3 to the Perform (comedy) check
DC +15 to +19	+4 to the Perform (comedy) check
DC +20 or more	+5 to the Perform (comedy) check

2. Skill Synergy

Perform (comedy) as Primary Skill: Acrobatics

Perform (comedy) as Synergy Skill: None

Perform (dance)

The following Synergy Skill may benefit the Perform (dance) skill.

Acrobatics—Surprise Moves

Extreme spins, rolls, leaps, and more can be added to one's dance, going far beyond the standard steps.

This Synergy Effect from Acrobatics only applies to Perform (dance) checks not confined to a rigid style and that do not have a partner (or, at least, one where the partner will not impede the acrobatic moves or can themselves participate.)

DC: Primary Skill DC + 5

Action: None; the acrobatics are integrated into the performance

Acrobatics—Surprise Moves

Check Result	Synergy Effect
DC -15 or lower	-4 to the Perform (dance) check
DC -10 to -14	-3 to the Perform (dance) check
DC -5 to -9	-2 to the Perform (dance) check
DC -1 to -4	-1 to the Perform (dance) check
DC +0 to +4	+1 to the Perform (dance) check
DC +5 to +9	+2 to the Perform (dance) check
DC +10 to +14	+3 to the Perform (dance) check
DC +15 to +19	+4 to the Perform (dance) check
DC +20 or more	+5 to the Perform (dance) check

Perform (dance) as Primary Skill: Acrobatics

Perform (dance) as Synergy Skill: None

Profession (various)

The following Synergy Skills may benefit a Profession skill.

Knowledge (various)—In the Know

The right body of knowledge can provide crucial information to a related profession.

This Synergy Effect from a Knowledge skill only applies to Profession checks the Gamemaster feels are appropriate. For example, Profession (courtesan) could certainly benefit from Knowledge (nobility) as a Synergy Skill but Profession (tanner) almost certainly would not.

DC: Primary Skill DC + 2d4

Action: 1 free action

Knowledge (various)—In the Know

Check Result	Synergy Effect
DC -15 or lower	-4 to the Profession (various) check
DC -10 to -14	-3 to the Profession (various) check
DC -5 to -9	-2 to the Profession (various) check
DC -1 to -4	-1 to the Profession (various) check
DC +0 to +4	+1 to the Profession (various) check
DC +5 to +9	+2 to the Profession (various) check
DC +10 to +14	+3 to the Profession (various) check
DC +15 to +19	+4 to the Profession (various) check
DC +20 or more	+5 to the Profession (various) check

Profession as Primary Skill: Knowledge (various)

Profession as Synergy Skill: None

Ride

The following Synergy Skill may benefit the Ride skill.

Handle Animal—Know Your Mount

Someone who is more familiar with raising, training, and handling animals is more likely to be able to get a mount to perform as desired and keep them under control.

DC: Primary Skill DC

Action: 1 free action

Handle Animal—Know Your Mount

Check Result	Synergy Effect
DC -15 or lower	-4 to the Ride check
DC -10 to -14	-3 to the Ride check
DC -5 to -9	-2 to the Ride check
DC -1 to -4	-1 to the Ride check
DC +0 to +4	+1 to the Ride check
DC +5 to +9	+2 to the Ride check
DC +10 to +14	+3 to the Ride check
DC +15 to +19	+4 to the Ride check
DC +20 or more	+5 to the Ride check

Ride as Primary Skill: Handle Animal

Ride as Synergy Skill: None

Sense Motive

The following Synergy Skills may benefit the Sense Motive skill.

Diplomacy—Spot the Tell

A competent diplomat will know what signs to look for when discerning someone's motives and intentions.

This Synergy Effect from Diplomacy only applies to Sense Motive checks regarding a hunch.

DC: Primary Skill DC + 5

Action: 1 free action

Diplomacy—Spot the Tell

Check Result	Synergy Effect
DC -15 or lower	−4 to the Sense Motive check
DC -10 to -14	−3 to the Sense Motive check
DC -5 to -9	−2 to the Sense Motive check
DC -1 to -4	−1 to the Sense Motive check
DC +0 to +4	+1 to the Sense Motive check
DC +5 to +9	+1 to the Sense Motive check and if successful make another DC 25 Sense Motive check * with success indicating you can discern what the NPC's attitude towards you is
DC +10 to +14	+2 to the Sense Motive check and if successful make another DC 25 Sense Motive check * with success indicating you can discern what the NPC's attitude towards you is
DC +15 to +19	+2 to the Sense Motive check and if successful make another DC 20 Sense Motive check * with success indicating you can discern what the NPC's attitude towards you is
DC +20 or more	+3 to the Sense Motive check and if successful make another DC 20 Sense Motive check * with success indicating you can discern what the NPC's attitude towards you is

* Do not add any synergy modifiers to this additional check

Perception—Gut Feeling

An aware person who follows his instincts may be able to better anticipate their subject's intentions.

This Synergy Effect from Perception only applies to Sense Motive checks regarding a hunch.

DC: Primary Skill DC + 5

Action: 1 free action

Perception—Gut Feeling

Check Result	Synergy Effect
DC -15 or lower	−2 to the Sense Motive check and failure means you suffer a -2 penalty to initiative if the subject initiates combat against you within one round
DC -10 to -14	−2 to the Sense Motive check and failure means you suffer a -1 penalty to initiative if the subject initiates combat against you within one round
DC -5 to -9	−1 to the Sense Motive check and failure means you suffer a -1 penalty to initiative if the subject initiates combat against you within one round
DC -1 to -4	−1 to the Sense Motive check
DC +0 to +4	+1 to the Sense Motive check
DC +5 to +9	+1 to the Sense Motive check and success means you gain a +1 circumstance bonus to initiative if the subject initiates combat against you within one round
DC +10 to +14	+2 to the Sense Motive check and success means you gain a +1 circumstance bonus to initiative if the subject initiates combat against you within one round
DC +15 to +19	+2 to the Sense Motive check and success means you gain a +2 circumstance bonus to initiative if the subject initiates combat against you within one round
DC +20 or more	+3 to the Sense Motive check and success means you gain a +2 circumstance bonus to initiative if the subject initiates combat against you within one round

Perception—Wink, Wink, Say No More

Someone with a keen eye is better able to notice abnormalities in someone's speech and behavior that conceal a hidden meaning.

This Synergy Effect from Perception only applies to Sense Motive checks to discern secret messages.

DC: Primary Skill DC + 2

Action: 1 free action

2. SKILL SYNERGY

Perception—Wink, Wink, Say No More

Check Result	Synergy Effect
DC -15 or lower	−2 to the Sense Motive check and failure by 5 or more means the wrong message will be very detrimental to the subject who misunderstood it, such as failing to show up at the correct location for a dangerous meeting where the subject was meant to act as backup
DC -10 to -14	−2 to the Sense Motive check and failure by 5 or more means the wrong message will be somewhat detrimental to the subject who misunderstood it, such as causing the subject to wear something inappropriate to an appointment
DC -5 to -9	−1 to the Sense Motive check and failure by 5 or more means the wrong message will be somewhat detrimental to the subject who misunderstood it, such as causing the subject to wear something inappropriate to an appointment
DC -1 to -4	−1 to the Sense Motive check
DC +0 to +4	+1 to the Sense Motive check
DC +5 to +9	+2 to the Sense Motive check
DC +10 to +14	+3 to the Sense Motive check
DC +15 to +19	+4 to the Sense Motive check
DC +20 or more	+5 to the Sense Motive check

Spellcraft—See the Signs

The sort of intuitive and trained knowledge represented by the Spellcraft skill can make the observer more aware of signs of enchantment when studying a subject's behavior.

This Synergy Effect from Spellcraft only applies to Sense Motive checks to sense enchantment.

DC: Primary Skill DC + 5

Action: 1 free acton

> **Sense Motive as Primary Skill:**
> Diplomacy, Perception, Spellcraft
>
> **Sense Motive as Synergy Skill:** Diplomacy, Perception

> **Sleight of Hand as Primary Skill:** Bluff
>
> **Sleight of Hand as Synergy Skill:** Escape Artist

Spellcraft—See the Signs

Check Result	Synergy Effect
DC -15 or lower	-4 to the Sense Motive check
DC -10 to -14	-3 to the Sense Motive check
DC -5 to -9	-2 to the Sense Motive check
DC -1 to -4	-1 to the Sense Motive check
DC +0 to +4	+1 to the Sense Motive check
DC +5 to +9	+2 to the Sense Motive check
DC +10 to +14	+3 to the Sense Motive check
DC +15 to +19	+4 to the Sense Motive check
DC +20 or more	+5 to the Sense Motive check

Sleight of Hand

The following Synergy Skills may benefit the Sleight of Hand skill.

Bluff—Confident Facade

When someone is observing you undertake an action you would rather conceal, a show of confidence, as though you do not care that anyone is watching you because you are not doing anything wrong, can be enough to distract the observer.

This Synergy Effect from Bluff only applies to Sleight of Hand checks to pick pockets, draw a hidden weapon, or hide something.

DC: Primary Skill DC + 5

Action: None

Bluff—Confident Facade

Check Result	Synergy Effect
DC -15 or lower	-3 to the Sleight of Hand check
DC -10 to -14	-3 to the Sleight of Hand check
DC -5 to -9	-2 to the Sleight of Hand check
DC -1 to -4	-1 to the Sleight of Hand check
DC +0 to +4	+1 to the Sleight of Hand check
DC +5 to +9	+2 to the Sleight of Hand check
DC +10 to +14	+3 to the Sleight of Hand check
DC +15 to +19	+4 to the Sleight of Hand check and you may use Sleight of Hand to take an object from another creature during combat even if that creature is aware of your presence
DC +20 or more	+5 to the Sleight of Hand check and you may use Sleight of Hand to take an object from another creature during combat even if that creature is aware of your presence

Spellcraft

The following Synergy Skill may benefit the Spellcraft skill.

Knowledge (arcana)—Lore of Mysteries

Understanding the fundamental mysteries of magic, in its raw and ritualized forms, makes one better able to work with and identify aspects of magic.

This Synergy Effect from Knowledge (arcana) does not apply to Spellcraft checks to craft a magic item.

DC: Primary Skill DC + 3

Action: 1 free action

Knowledge (arcana)—Lore of Mysteries

Check Result	Synergy Effect
DC -15 or lower	-4 to the Spellcraft check and if the Spellcraft check fails the time required before a learn a spell from a spellbook or scroll retry may be made is increased to 2 weeks and to prepare a spell from a borrowed spellbook retry is increased to 2 days
DC -10 to -14	-3 to the Spellcraft check and if the Spellcraft check fails the time required before a learn a spell from a spellbook or scroll retry may be made is increased to 11 days and to prepare a spell from a borrowed spellbook retry is increased to 36 hours
DC -5 to -9	-2 to the Spellcraft check
DC -1 to -4	-1 to the Spellcraft check
DC +0 to +4	+1 to the Spellcraft check
DC +5 to +9	+2 to the Spellcraft check
DC +10 to +14	+3 to the Spellcraft check
DC +15 to +19	+4 to the Spellcraft check and if the Spellcraft check fails the time required before a learn a spell from a spellbook or scroll retry may be made is reduced to 4 days and to prepare a spell from a borrowed spellbook retry is reduced to 12 hours
DC +20 or more	+5 to the Spellcraft check and if the Spellcraft check fails the time required before a learn a spell from a spellbook or scroll retry may be made is reduced to 2 days and to prepare a spell from a borrowed spellbook retry is reduced to 6 hours

Use Magic Device—Scroll Reader

Understanding how to activate a spell scroll can make one more capable of decrypting its arcane contents without activating its magic.

This Synergy Effect from Use Magic Device only applies to Spellcraft checks to decipher a scroll.

DC: Primary Skill DC + 7

Action: 1 free action

Use Magic Device—Scroll Reader

Check Result	Synergy Effect
DC -15 or lower	-4 to the Spellcraft check and if the Spellcraft check fails the time required before a decipher a scroll retry may be made is increased to 2 weeks
DC -10 to -14	-3 to the Spellcraft check and if the Spellcraft check fails the time required before a decipher a scroll retry may be made is increased to 11 days
DC -5 to -9	-2 to the Spellcraft check
DC -1 to -4	-1 to the Spellcraft check
DC +0 to +4	+1 to the Spellcraft check
DC +5 to +9	+2 to the Spellcraft check
DC +10 to +14	+3 to the Spellcraft check
DC +15 to +19	+4 to the Spellcraft check and if the Spellcraft check fails the time required before a decipher a scroll retry may be made is reduced to 4 days
DC +20 or more	+5 to the Spellcraft check and if the Spellcraft check fails the time required before a decipher a scroll retry may be made is reduced to 2 days

Spellcraft as Primary Skill:
Knowledge (arcana), Use Magic Device

Spellcraft as Synergy Skill:
Sense Motive, Use Magic Device

Survival

The following Synergy Skills may benefit the Survival skill.

Knowledge (dungeoneering)—Tunnel Rat

Awareness and understanding of the creatures and plant life that flourishes in the tunnels and caverns beneath the surface, including the natural hazards posed by them, may increase one's chance of surviving such a dangerous environment.

2. Skill Synergy

This Synergy Effect from Knowledge (dungeoneering) only applies to Survival checks made while underground.

DC: Primary Skill DC + 7

Action: 1 free action

Knowledge (dungeoneering)—Tunnel Rat

Check Result	Synergy Effect
DC -15 or lower	-4 to the Survival check and a retry for getting along in the wild can only be made 3 days after a previous failure
DC -10 to -14	-3 to the Survival check and a retry for getting along in the wild can only be made 2 days after a previous failure
DC -5 to -9	-2 to the Survival check
DC -1 to -4	-1 to the Survival check
DC +0 to +4	+1 to the Survival check
DC +5 to +9	+1 to the Survival check
DC +10 to +14	+2 to the Survival check
DC +15 to +19	+2 to the Survival check and a retry for getting along in the wild can be attempted within 18 hours of a previous failure
DC +20 or more	+3 to the Survival check and a retry for getting along in the wild can be attempted within 12 hours of a previous failure

Knowledge (geography)—Lay of the Land

Better understanding of how terrain is formed, is affected by climate, and so on may allow one to better discern one's location and know how to spot danger posed by the landscape, such as sinkholes, rockslides, and areas that are likely susceptible to avalanches.

This Synergy Effect from Knowledge (geography) only applies to Survival checks to keep from getting lost or to avoid natural hazards.

DC: Primary Skill DC + 5

Action: 1 free action

Knowledge (geography)—Lay of the Land

Check Result	Synergy Effect
DC -15 or lower	-4 to the Survival check
DC -10 to -14	-3 to the Survival check
DC -5 to -9	-2 to the Survival check
DC -1 to -4	-1 to the Survival check
DC +0 to +4	+1 to the Survival check
DC +5 to +9	+2 to the Survival check
DC +10 to +14	+3 to the Survival check
DC +15 to +19	+4 to the Survival check
DC +20 or more	+5 to the Survival check

Knowledge (nature)—Wilderness Awareness

Better understanding of the flora, fauna, seasons, and weather common to the great outdoors makes it easier for one to survive such elements.

Knowledge (nature)—Wilderness Awareness

Check Result	Synergy Effect
DC -15 or lower	-3 to the Survival check and any Fortitude save bonus vs resulting severe weather is increased to +0 (+2 if stationary)
DC -10 to -14	-2 to the Survival check and any Fortitude save bonus vs resulting severe weather is increased to +1 (+3 if stationary)
DC -5 to -9	-2 to the Survival check
DC -1 to -4	-1 to the Survival check
DC +0 to +4	+1 to the Survival check
DC +5 to +9	+1 to the Survival check and any Fortitude save bonus vs resulting severe weather is increased to +3 (+5 if stationary)
DC +10 to +14	+2 to the Survival check and any Fortitude save bonus vs resulting severe weather is increased to +3 (+5 if stationary)
DC +15 to +19	+2 to the Survival check and any Fortitude save bonus vs resulting severe weather is increased to +4 (+6 if stationary)
DC +20 or more	+3 to the Survival check and any Fortitude save bonus vs resulting severe weather is increased to +4 (+6 if stationary)

This Synergy Effect from Knowledge (nature) only applies to Survival checks in aboveground natural environments (aquatic, desert, forest, hill, marsh, mountains, and plains.)

DC: Primary Skill DC + 2

Action: 1 free action

Knowledge (planes) —Otherworldly Awareness

Other planes of existence are usually radically different with regards to terrain, climate, weather, and flora and fauna, making the application of a survival techniques standard to one's native planes problematic. However, someone who has studied these other worlds may be more capable of handling whatever these varied environments has in store for them.

This Synergy Effect from Knowledge (planes) only applies to Survival checks made while on planes of existence the character is not native to.

DC: Primary Skill DC + 7

Action: 1 free action

Knowledge (planes)—Otherworldly Awareness

Check Result	Synergy Effect
DC -15 or lower	-4 to the Survival check and a retry for getting along in the wild can only be made 3 days after a previous failure
DC -10 to -14	-3 to the Survival check and a retry for getting along in the wild can only be made 2 days after a previous failure
DC -5 to -9	-2 to the Survival check
DC -1 to -4	-1 to the Survival check
DC +0 to +4	+1 to the Survival check
DC +5 to +9	+1 to the Survival check
DC +10 to +14	+2 to the Survival check
DC +15 to +19	+2 to the Survival check and a retry for getting along in the wild can be attempted within 18 hours of a previous failure
DC +20 or more	+3 to the Survival check and a retry for getting along in the wild can be attempted within 12 hours of a previous failure

2. Skill Synergy

Perception—Spot the Trail

Someone with a good eye for detail may be better able to find tracks and follow them after finding indicators other, less observant trackers might miss.

This Synergy Effect from Perception only applies to Survival checks to find or follow tracks.

DC: Primary Skill DC

Action: 1 full-round action

Perception—Spot the Trail

Check Result	Synergy Effect
DC -15 or lower	-4 to the Survival check and a retry can only be attempted after 8 hours (outdoors) / 80 minutes (indoors) following a previous failure
DC -10 to -14	-3 to the Survival check and a retry can only be attempted after 4 hours (outdoors) / 40 minutes (indoors) following a previous failure
DC -5 to -9	-2 to the Survival check and a retry can only be attempted after 2 hours (outdoors) / 20 minutes (indoors) following a previous failure
DC -1 to -4	-1 to the Survival check
DC +0 to +4	+1 to the Survival check
DC +5 to +9	+2 to the Survival check
DC +10 to +14	+3 to the Survival check and a retry can be attempted within 30 minutes (outdoors) / 5 minutes (indoors) of a previous failure
DC +15 to +19	+4 to the Survival check and a retry can be attempted within 15 minutes (outdoors) / 2 minutes (indoors) of a previous failure
DC +20 or more	+5 to the Survival check and a retry can be attempted within 15 minutes (outdoors) / 1 round (indoors) of a previous failure

Survival as Primary Skill: Knowledge (dungeoneering), Knowledge (geography), Knowledge (nature), Knowledge (planes), Perception

Survival as Synergy Skill: Knowledge (nature)

Use Magic Device

The following Synergy Skills may benefit the Use Magic Device skill.

Linguistics—Read Spell Scroll

Carefully studying a spell scroll before using it may provide a better chance of reading its mysterious script properly.

This Synergy Effect from Linguistics only applies to Use Magic Device checks for the use a scroll skill ability.

DC: Primary Skill DC

Action: 1d10 rounds

Linguistics—Read Spell Scroll

Check Result	Synergy Effect
DC -15 or lower	-4 to the Use Magic Device check and casting a spell from a scroll requires a minimum score (15 + spell level) in the appropriate ability
DC -10 to -14	-3 to the Use Magic Device check and casting a spell from a scroll requires a minimum score (13 + spell level) in the appropriate ability
DC -5 to -9	-2 to the Use Magic Device check and casting a spell from a scroll requires a minimum score (11 + spell level) in the appropriate ability
DC -1 to -4	-1 to the Use Magic Device check
DC +0 to +4	+1 to the Use Magic Device check
DC +5 to +9	+1 to the Use Magic Device check and casting a spell from a scroll requires a minimum score (8 + spell level) in the appropriate ability
DC +10 to +14	+2 to the Use Magic Device check and casting a spell from a scroll requires a minimum score (8 + spell level) in the appropriate ability
DC +15 to +19	+2 to the Use Magic Device check and casting a spell from a scroll requires a minimum score (5 + spell level) in the appropriate ability
DC +20 or more	You may take 10 with the Use Magic Device check and casting a spell from a scroll requires a minimum score (5 + spell level) in the appropriate ability

Spellcraft—Decrypt Scroll

Being intimately familiar with identifying and analyzing spells and magic scrolls can make untangling their mysteries somewhat easier.

This Synergy Effect from Spellcraft only applies to Use Magic Device checks to decipher a written spell from a scroll.

DC: Primary Skill DC + 7

Action: 1 free action

Use Magic Device as Primary Skill: Linguistics, Spellcraft

Use Magic Device as Synergy Skill: Spellcraft

Spellcraft—Decrypt Scroll

Check Result	Synergy Effect
DC -15 or lower	-4 to the Use Magic Device and the decipher a written spell process takes 5 minutes of concentration
DC -10 to -14	-3 to the Use Magic Device and the decipher a written spell process takes 2 minutes of concentration
DC -5 to -9	-2 to the Use Magic Device check
DC -1 to -4	-1 to the Use Magic Device check
DC +0 to +4	+1 to the Use Magic Device check
DC +5 to +9	+2 to the Use Magic Device check
DC +10 to +14	+3 to the Use Magic Device check
DC +15 to +19	+4 to the Use Magic Device check and the decipher a written spell process takes 30 seconds (6 rounds) of concentration
DC +20 or more	+5 to the Use Magic Device check and the decipher a written spell process takes 15 seconds (3 rounds) of concentration

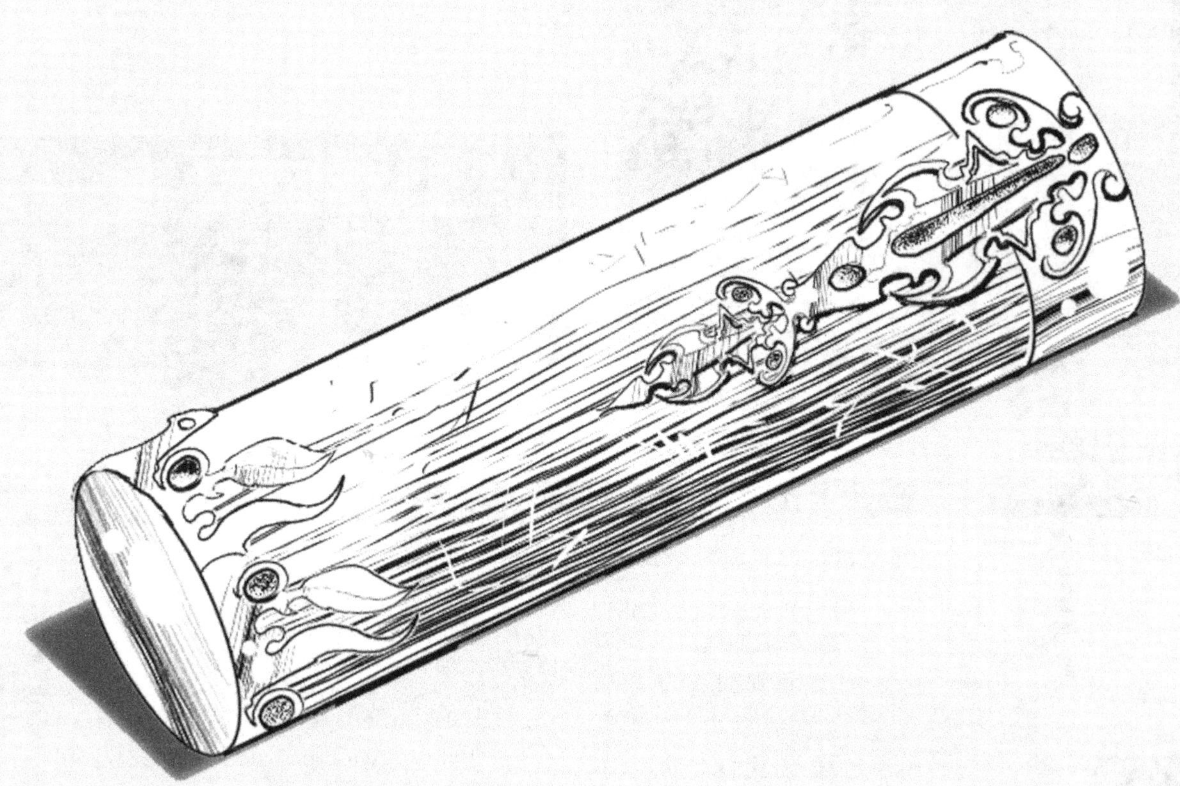

Chapter 3

Feat Synergy

any feats are inherently designed to interact with skills, usually by providing them with bonuses that apply in all or limited capacities within which the skill may be employed. However, for the most part they are not intended to interact with each other beyond instances where some feats stand as prerequisites for others or improve the benefits provided by other feats. With the inclusion of Feat Synergy, the advantages some feats bestow may now overlap and interact with each other in related ways in order to grant additional abilities or allow for spectacular maneuvers and deeds. Much like feats, however, each instance of Feat Synergy also has prerequisites that must be met.

Gamemaster are encouraged to use the following as examples from which to design their own Synergy Effects for feats, especially when using third-party feats not covered in the **Pathfinder® Roleplaying Game Core Rulebook™**, **Pathfinder® Roleplaying Game: Advanced Player's Guide™**, **Pathfinder® Roleplaying Game: Ultimate Magic™**, and **Pathfinder® Roleplaying Game: Ultimate Combat™**.

Using Feat Synergy in your games will introduce an entirely new level of possibilities.

Feat Synergy and Game Balance

In a way, allowing synergy between feats acts as an additional feat unto itself. If you feel Feat Synergy treads too closely to replacing feats, simply ignore it and be content with the other synergy-related content found in this product. You can also require a character purchase each Feat Synergy Effect as its own feat using the Feat Synergy Effect's name.

Terms of Feat Synergy

Prerequisites: The feats required to work together in order to obtain the desired Feat Synergy Effect.

Synergy Effect: The desired benefit or maneuver obtained by using the specified feats together.

Feat Synergy Effects

Name	Prerequisites	Synergy Effect
Adamantine Lungs	Athletic, Endurance, Great Fortitude	You can hold your breath 50% longer than normal
Appealing Leader	Leadership, Persuasive, Sociable ᵅ, Voice of the Sibyl ᵘ	+1 to Leadership
Archer's Wall	Missile Shield ᵅ, Point-Blank Shot, Precise Shot, Shield Focus, Shield Proficiency	Gain a +1 bonus to AC for your shield, as well as damage reduction, against arrows and crossbow bolts
Avoid Sneak Attack	Acrobatic, Alertness, Lightning Reflexes	Make an Acrobatics check to move out of the way and avoid taking extra damage from a sneak attack
Bait and Strike	Combat Expertise, Deceptive, Disengaging Feint ᵠ, Improved Feint	Roll twice for the first attack of a full attack, full-round action

Feat Synergy Effects, continued

Name	Prerequisites	Synergy Effect
Block and Counter	Combat Expertise, Combat Reflexes, Weapon Specialisation, and Improved Disarm *or* Improved Trip	An attack missing you by 5 or more may allow you an attack of opportunity
Body Flip	Athletic, Improved Grapple, Improved Trip	Grapple an opponent to throw him to the ground hard
Chosen Weapon	Greater Weapon Focus, Power Attack, Weapon Focus, Weapon Specialization	Beat your foe's AC by 10 or more to inflict additional damage
Clear Some Space	Combat Expertise, Dodge, Improved Disarm, Mobility, Spring Attack, Whirlwind Attack	Instead of doing harm with a whirlwind attack you can force opponents to take a step back
Confined Trick Attack	Acrobatics, Acrobatic Steps, Nimble Moves, Step Up	Use Acrobatics to catch your opponent by surprise in a confined area, rendering him flat-footed against you
Countercharge	Mobility, Run, Step-Up	Use a Delay action to charge an opponent who is charging you, negating his charge's attack bonus
Desperate Dodge	Acrobatic, Agile Maneuvers, Dodge	An Acrobatics check may allow you to retain your Dodge bonus when you lose your Dex bonus to AC
Distraction	Deft Hands, Persuasive	A successful Bluff allows you to add your Charisma bonus to Sleight of Hand checks
Dive for Cover	Improved Initiative, Lightning Reflexes, Quick Draw	If surprised you may attempt a Reflex save to make a move action
Enduring Swimmer	Athletic, Endurance, Skill Focus (Swim)	You may take a standard action while holding your breath by making a Constitution check
Guarded Caster	Combat Casting, Spell Focus, Spell Mastery	An appropriate spell is not lost if you fail a *casting defensively* concentration check
Headsman's Stroke	Combat Expertise, Combat Reflexes, Critical Focus, Vital Strike	A critical hit during an attack of opportunity may result in your opponent's decapitation
Heave	Athletic, Great Fortitude, Toughness	Temporarily increase your Strength for carrying, lifting, and dragging
High Diver	Acrobatic, Athletic, Skill Focus (Swim)	Falling or diving into water is less likely to be harmful
Leaping Lunge	Acrobatic, Lunge, Power Attack	Double your Power Attack modifiers while performing a Lunge and leaping
Limber Wrestler	Acrobatic, Dodge, Improved Unarmed Strike, Improved Grapple, Mobility	Substitute Acrobatics ranks for your Strength modifier when opposing a grapple
Low Charge	Charge Through ᵠ, Dodge, Mobility, Power Attack	+2 to damage while charging but provokes an attack of opportunity
Open Defense	Combat Reflexes, Deceitful, Improved Feint	Make an opening in your defenses for your opponent in order to obtain an attack of opportunity against him
Oversized Mount	Acrobatic, Animal Affinity, Athletic	*Fast mount or dismount* a mount up to two size categories larger

ᵃ See the *Pathfinder® Roleplaying Game: Advanced Player's Guide™*
ᵘ See the *Pathfinder® Roleplaying Game: Ultimate Magic™*
ᵠ See the *Pathfinder® Roleplaying Game: Ultimate Combat™*

3. feat synergy

Feat Synergy Effects, continued

Name	Prerequisites	Synergy Effect
Oversized Rush	Improved Bull Rush, Improved Grapple, Improved Unarmed Strike, Power Attack	You may bull rush creatures up to two sizes larger
Rampaging Whirlwind	Acrobatic, Combat Expertise, Combat Reflexes, Dodge, Mobility, Spring Attack, Whirlwind Attack	Take a 5-foot step and continue your Whirlwind Attack from that new position
Ranged Disarm	Combat Expertise, Improved Disarm, Improved Precise Shot, Point-Blank Shot, Precise Shot	Attempt to disarm a target with a ranged weapon by accepting a −8 penalty to the roll Ritualize Spell
Rolling Rider	Acrobatic, Animal Affinity	Reduce damage when falling from a mount
Second Guess	Alertness, Deceitful, Persuasive	Make Sense Motive and Bluff checks to change the mind of someone not convinced by your disguise
Shield Rush	Improved Bull Rush, Improved Shield Bash, Power Attack, Shield Proficiency	Use your shield during a bull rush to gain +2 CMB with a light shield or +4 with a heavy shield
Staggering Blow	Bludgeoner [ϙ], Dazing Assault [α], Weapon Focus	Use a blunt weapon or the flat of a blade to cause an opponent to be *staggered* rather than inflict damage
Steady Step	Acrobatic, Acrobatic Steps, Nimble Moves	Reduce Acrobatics skill conditional modifiers
Stop Charge	Deadly Aim, Vital Strike, Weapon Focus	Make a ranged attack as a readied action in order to stop an opponent's charge
Sure Grip	Acrobatic, Athletic, Skill Focus (Climb)	Reduced DCs to catch yourself on a slope or wall while falling
Swinging Attack	Athletic, Combat Expertise, Nimble Moves	Bull rush, melee attack, or trip an opponent while swinging from an object
Treasonous Dodge	Agile Maneuvers, Dodge, Flanking Foil [ϙ], Mobility, Spring Attack	You make a Reflex saving throw to trick flanking opponents into attacking each other instead of you
Vault Opponent	Acrobatic, Agile Maneuvers, Sidestep [α], Step Up	Leap over your opponent, landing beside or behind him, in order to make a surprise attack
Whirling Deflection	Combat Reflexes, Deflect Arrows, Improved Unarmed Strike, Lightning Reflexes	You may roll Reflex saving throws to attempt more than one ranged attack deflection
Whirling Return	Combat Reflexes, Deflect Arrows, Improved Unarmed Strike, Lightning Reflexes, Snatch Arrows	Multiple snatched thrown weapons may be immediately thrown or kept
Whistling Shot	Alertness, Blind-Fight, Improved Blind-Fight [α]	Make a (DC +5) Perception check to negate a ranged attacker's invisibility benefits

Adamantine Lungs

Pushing your body to its limits has its benefits when it comes to optimizing its use of oxygen.

Prerequisites: Athletic, Endurance, Great Fortitude

You can hold your breath 50% longer than normal.

Appealing Leader

Your combined aptitudes for creating and manipulating social relationships make people more likely to follow your cause.

Prerequisites: Leadership, Persuasive, Sociable [α], Voice of the Sibyl [μ]

You gain a +1 bonus to your Leadership score.

Archer's Wall

Your own experiences as an archer has taught you how to best position your shield to intercept incoming projectile or thrown attacks.

Prerequisites: Missile Shield [α], Point-Blank Shot, Precise Shot, Shield Focus, Shield Proficiency

While moving no more than half your normal distance during a move action and while not in melee combat, you gain a +1 competence bonus to AC with your shield and apply your shield's normal AC bonus as damage reduction against a ranged attack with sling stones, thrown objects, arrows, crossbow bolts, and similar projectiles (and old fashioned, black powder fireamrs in games that allow them.) For example, a heavy wooden shield would grant damage reduction 2.

Avoid Sneak Attack

Even when caught by surprise, you may still attempt to escape taking additional damage from a sneak attack.

Prerequisites: Acrobatic, Alertness, Lightning Reflexes

When subjected to a sneak attack when you are not flat-footed but are otherwise not normally able to defend yourself against the attack, you may attempt a (DC 10 + attack roll against you) Acrobatics skill check as a move action. If you succeed, you are able to move 5 feet in any direction that is not currently occupied without drawing an attack of opportunity. Success reduces the sneak attack to normal damage. However, failing the Acrobatics check means that if the sneak attack hits you it does the usual sneak attack damage and you also provoke an attack of opportunity from anyone other than the sneak attacker who is in a position to do so.

If you cannot move into an unoccupied space within 5 feet, you cannot use Avoid Sneak Attack.

Bait and Strike

Misdirection allows you to feint a strike to one area of your target but reverse your attack in order to strike at another location.

Prerequisites: Combat Expertise, Deceptive, Disengaging Feint φ, Improved Feint

When conducting a full attack as a full-round action, you roll to attack twice for the first strike, using the higher roll if your opponent fails a Sense Motive check. The Sense Motive check'sDC is equal to the highest of these two attack rolls. If the Sense Motive check succeeds you instead use the lowest of the two attack rolls. Following attacks are rolled normally.

You must be wearing light or no armour to employ this Feat Synergy Effect.

Block and Counter

After you parry an opponent's attack you can create an opening for a quick counterattack.

Prerequisites: Combat Expertise, Combat Reflexes, Weapon Specialisation, and Improved Disarm *or* Improved Trip

When you are utilizing Combat Expertise with a weapon with which you are specialized, an attack against you that fails to defeat your AC by 5 or more allows you to immediately initiate an attack of opportunity to make your choice of the usual melee attack, or a disarm (if you have Improved Disarm) or trip (if you have Improved Trip.)

This disarm or trip attempt suffers from your Combat Expertise penalty and counts against your total number of attacks of opportunity for that round.

3. feat synergy

Body Flip

Using strength, leverage, and combat experience, you can flip your opponent onto the ground.

Prerequisites: Athletic, Improved Grapple, Improved Trip

If you have at least one hand free to do so, make a grapple against your opponent. If successful, instead of one of the usual grapple results you throw him to the ground. Such an opponent suffers damage as though from an unarmed attack from you and is prone as though tripped. The opponent is no longer considered grappled.

Chosen Weapon

You have a near total familiarity with your weapon, allowing you to better penetrate a foe's defenses in order to cause greater harm.

Prerequisites: Greater Weapon Focus, Power Attack, Weapon Focus, Weapon Specialization

When using the weapon to which Weapon Focus, Weapon Specialization, and Greater Weapon Focus apply, a successful attack inflicts additional damage if the attack roll is higher than the target's AC by 10 or more. For example, rolling a 25 or higher to strike a target with an AC of 15 would inflict the additional damage.

Normal Damage	Additional Damage
1d3 or less	1 point
1d4	1 point
1d6	1d2
1d8	1d2
2d4	1d3
1d10	1d4
1d12	1d4
2d6	1d4
2d8	1d6
3d6	1d6
2d10	1d8
3d8	1d10
4d8	2d6

The amount of additional damage depends on the damage the weapon normally causes.

This damage is always added after additional damage modifiers have been accounted for, such as a critical hit multiplier.

Clear Some Space

Instead of using your combat expertise to inflict harm, you may use it to clear yourself enough room to try and escape when outnumbered.

Prerequisites: Combat Expertise, Dodge, Improved Disarm, Mobility, Spring Attack, Whirlwind Attack

Instead of seeking to cause harm while making a whirlwind attack, you instead sweep your weapon all about you, forcing any opponent within 5 feet to take a 5-foot step away from you. This counts as a free action for them. Any opponent who chooses not to step away (or cannot) is instead subjected to a whirlwind attack, as normal.

Employing this Synergy Effect requires at least five squares adjacent to you be occupied by opponents, and you cannot be using a finesse weapon to do so.

Confined Trick Attack

You are skilled at using an enclosed, cramped area to aid your attacks in an unorthodox manner.

Prerequisites: Acrobatics, Acrobatic Steps, Nimble Moves, Step Up

You may attempt an unusual, extraordinary attack while fighting in a tight area, such as a tunnel or in a building. Describes how you make the attack by using the environment, such as leaping off a table and into a doorway, bracing yourself with your legs while slashing downward into an opponent. Regardless of what is described, it counts as a full-round action to account for the move and attack (using a move action and standard action, respectively.)

Roll an Acrobatics check, the DC of which is your opponent's attack roll. Your opponent is considered flat-footed against the attack if successful (but not against other attacks against him.) In other regards, conduct the attack against this foe normally. You may still attack if the Acrobatics check fails, but suffer a -2 penalty to do so.

Countercharge

You rush out to meet on your own terms an enemy charging you with an attack of your own.

Prerequisites: Mobility, Run, Step-Up

When an enemy declares a charge against you while you are on a Delay action (you cannot use a Ready action, as that uses a standard action of its own), you can announce a Countercharge. You move toward the charging enemy even as they move toward you, stopping roughly halfway between your two starting positions. The enemy then makes his attack, but does not gain any bonuses from charging, although the AC penalties still apply. If you are still able to, you may then make your own charge attack as normal.

Lastly, your initiative result is modified to one less than that of the enemy you countercharged.

Desperate Dodge

The ability to twist, turn, and spin your body about means you may still be able to better position yourself out of harm's way even if your reflexes are not as sharp as normal.

Prerequisites: Acrobatic, Agile Maneuvers, Dodge

When attacked during circumstances that would normally deny you your Dex bonus to AC, and thus also your Dodge bonus, make an Acrobatics check as a free action using the attack's roll result as the DC. You retain your Dodge bonus to AC if the check succeeds, but if the check fails your usual Dodge AC bonus is instead applied to your AC as a penalty.

Distraction

Sometimes knowing how to make the most of your personality can keep people from watching what you are doing with your hands.

Prerequisites: Deft Hands, Persuasive

Obtain an additional circumstance bonus equal to your Charisma bonus to Sleight of Hand checks against that subject in your next immediate action if you make a successful Bluff check against them.

Dive for Cover

Even when surprised, sometimes you can still feel danger at your back and know enough to be elsewhere.

Prerequisites: Improved Initiative, Lightning Reflexes, Quick Draw

Although you remain flat-footed with regards to your Dex bonus' influence on your AC if caught unaware during a surprise round, you may attempt a Reflex save using your opponents' highest initiative roll as the DC. If this saving throw succeeds, you are allowed a single move action during the surprise round.

Enduring Swimmer

Honing your body and working hard to become a skilled swimmer can make functioning in water seem more natural.

Prerequisites: Athletic, Endurance, Skill Focus (Swim)

You can make a single standard action with no other actions in a round when you are holding your breath without losing an additional 1 round of breath, as would normally be the case. You do this if you succeed at a (DC 10 + previous rounds you've already held your breath for) Constitution check as a free action. You cannot even take free actions other than that required of the Constitution check if attempting Enduring Swimmer.

Guarded Caster

Exceptional familiarity with a given spell allows you to retain its use if your concentration is broken.

Prerequisites: Combat Casting, Spell Focus, Spell Mastery

If the spell you are *casting defensively* is covered by Spell Mastery and is of a school you have Spell Focus for, you do not lose the spell if you fail the concentration check to cast on the defensive. Instead, the spell merely fails without further consequences.

Headsman's Stroke

Although doing so leaves you open to a counterattack, you may take advantage of weaknesses in your opponent's defences in order to cut his head clean off.

Prerequisites: Combat Expertise, Combat Reflexes, Critical Focus, Vital Strike

If you choose to employ this Synergy Effect while obtaining a critical hit with an attack of opportunity, your opponent must roll a (DC 5 + total damage) Fortitude saving throw. Your opponent's head is cut off and he is slain if he fails the saving throw. You suffer a -4 circumstance penalty to your AC for the one round immediately following your attack of opportunity if you choose to employ this Synergy Effect whether the saving throw fails or not.

The Gamemaster may rule this Synergy Effect may not be used in some circumstances, such as if the opponent is so tall its head is not within reach of the attack.

Heave

Your dedication to improving your physique temporarily allows you to lift more than is normal.

Prerequisties: Athletic, Great Fortitude, Toughness

A successful Strength check means you temporarily increase your Strength by 2 for the round, but only with regards to what you can carry, drag, and lift. You must make a DC 15 Fortitude saving throw in the following round or become *fatigued* for one round. You cannot employ Heave in back-to-back rounds or while *fatigued* or *exhausted*.

High Diver

Your athleticism and acrobatic agility may allow you to reduce the risk of harm when falling or deliberately diving into water.

Prerequisites: Acrobatic, Athletic, Skill Focus (Swim)

A fall into water that is at least 10 feet deep does no damage for the first 50 feet of the fall, and damage is risked in increments of 25 feet after that. The DC of the check made for deliberately diving into water only increases by 2 for every 50 feet of the dive.

Leaping Lunge

You leap into the air and forward, using your momentum to deliver a more powerful strike.

Prerequisites: Acrobatic, Lunge, Power Attack

By leaping up and extending towards your target, as per the Lunge feat, you can make a Power Attack. The maximum penalties and benefits of the Power Attack are double normal, however, and the usual AC penalty is doubled to -4. Doing so requires you make a (DC equal to opponent's AC) Acrobatics check, with failure indicating you do not gain the benefits of the Lunge or Power Attack, but still suffer the usual -2 penalty to AC for the lunge.

Limber Wrestler

Acrobatics has taught you how to twist and bend your body in unexpected ways, opening new possibilities for escaping a grapple that does not rely upon brute strength.

Prerequisites: Acrobatic, Dodge, Improved Unarmed Strike, Improved Grapple, Mobility

Substitute your Acrobatics ranks for your Strength modifier when performing a combat maneuver check opposing a grapple. Do not add your Dex modifier or the benefits from any feats or the like (other than Acrobatic) to your Acrobatics' rank for this purpose; only your "naked" Acrobatics ranks and the Acrobatic feat bonus apply. The exception is any enhancement bonus to Acrobatics, as magical items and the like may improve your chance of success.

Low Charge

A low charge can get you under your enemy's guard to stab deep into his belly with a blade. Doing so leaves you vulnerable to a counterattack.

Prerequisites: Charge Through ª, Dodge, Mobility, Power Attack

You gain a +2 bonus on your damage roll when charging with a slashing or piercing weapon, but you provoke an attack of opportunity from your target before you can make your attack roll.

Open Defense

Instead of defending against your opponent's weapon, you create an opening for him that also makes him weaken his defenses.

Prerequisites: Combat Reflexes, Deceitful, Improved Feint

Your attacker gains a +4 circumstance bonus to his attack roll. You may immediately make an attack of opportunity against him if he misses.

You cannot employ this Synergy Effect if you are flat-footed.

Oversized Mount

Your exceptional sense of balance, limberness, athleticism, and way with animals allows you to leap to and from the saddle of larger beasts.

Prerequisites: Acrobatic, Animal Affinity, Athletic

You can use *fast mount* of *dismount* (see the Ride skill) on a mount up to two size categories larger than yourself.

Oversized Rush

You know how to use your body to get greater than normal performance out of your size and mass.

Prerequisites: Improved Bull Rush, Improved Grapple, Improved Unarmed Strike, Power Attack

You may bull rush an opponent who is two size categories larger than you, the same size, or smaller.

3. Feat Synergy

Rampaging Whirlwind

While whirling your blades about you in a potentially devastating attack, you are not rooted in one place and are instead able to move around thanks to your previous experiences with such mobile combat techniques.

Prerequisites: Acrobatic, Combat Expertise, Combat Reflexes, Dodge, Mobility, Spring Attack, Whirlwind Attack

You may make a normal Whirlwind Attack, follow it up with a 5-foot step, and then attack all *new* targets within range of that spot as part of the same Whirlwind Attack. Doing so requires a DC 20 Acrobatics check as a free action when the time comes to take the 5-foot step.

Failure means you cannot take the 5-foot step, your actions end for that round, and you leave yourself somewhat open to attack. You suffer an AC penalty equal to the amount you failed the Acrobatics check by. This AC penalty lasts until your next action.

You cannot attack the same target twice with a Rampaging Whirlwind if a target is within reach of both your original and secondary positions.

Ranged Disarm

Such is your experience with attacking at range, you are able to use ranged attacks to try and remove an opponent's weapon from his grip.

Prerequisites: Combat Expertise, Improved Disarm, Improved Precise Shot, Point-Blank Shot, Precise Shot

To attempt a disarm using a ranged weapon attack instead of the usual melee attack, roll to disarm as normal but with a –8 penalty. If the disarm attempt fails by 10 or more, the disarming character does not drop his ranged weapon.

Ritualize Spell

By adding a more extensive, complex ritual process to your spells, you enhance their potency.

Prerequisites: Maximize Spell, Skill Focus (Knowledge: Arcana), Skill Focus (Spellcraft), Spell Focus (any)

You increase the degree of (or entirely add) ritualization to a spell in order to increase your effective caster level. This involves including more material components and increasing the casting time with new or added somantic and verbal components as a way to better focus the magic. (This entirely adds verbal and somantic components if the spell does not normally include them.)

Each step up on the accompanying tables one takes regarding the spell's casting time and/or material components, the spell's effective potency is increased by one caster level. However, successfully conducting the ritual is contingent upon making a DC 10 Spellcraft check at the ritual's end, increasing the DC by +5 for every increase in caster level you are attempting. If the check succeeds, the spell is cast at its enhanced level. Failure means the spell is not cast but will still count as having been cast so far as your available spell slots or the like are concerned.

Ritual Casting Time

Original Casting Time	New Casting Time
1 free / 1 swift / 1 immediate action	1 standard action
1 standard action	1 round
1 round	1 minute
1 round+ to 1 minute	10 minutes
1 minute+ to 10 minutes	1 hour
11 minutes to 1 hour or more	Multiply the original casting time by (1 + 1d4)

Ritual Material Components

Original Materials Value	New Materials Value
Less than 1 gp to 50 gp	100 gp
51 to 100 gp	250 gp
101 to 250 gp	500 gp
101 to 500 gp	750 gp
501 to 750 gp	1,000 gp
751 gp to 1,000 gp	Double the original value
More than 1,000 gp	Multiply the original value by (2 + 1d4)

For example, a wizard casting stoneskin *wishes to employ Ritualize Spell in order to make the spell last longer (duration being the spell's only caster level-determined element.) He chooses to attempt boosting the spell four caster levels by increasing the normal casting time of 1 standard action two steps and likewise increasing the material cost by two steps from 250 gp. To sucessfully cast the spell as a ritual, the wizard will now need to spend 10 minutes casting, use 1,000 gp worth of diamond dust, and make a DC 30 Spellcraft check.*

Ritualized spells are subject to the usual arcane spell failure, interruption, and similar conditions that would potentially influence the caster and/or spell. Additionally, you cannot move more than 5 feet from your starting point while using Ritualize Spell. Doing so disrupts the spell as though failing a concentration check against interruption.

Bards and Alchemists cannot makes use of Ritualize Spell. Obviously, using Ritualize Spell on certain spells is not going to be practical in some circumstances. Ritualizing a spell intended for the fast-paced action of combat, such as a fireball, for instance, would not make much sense unless the caster can be defended long enough to complete the ritual.

Rolling Rider

Your acrobatic experience grants you the chance to roll with, and thus reduce, any possible harm that may come from falling from your mount.

Prerequisites: Acrobatic, Animal Affinity

You only suffer 1d4 damage if you fail a soft fall Ride check or when falling while trying to make your mount leap.

Second Guess

Your understanding of others, mixed with your ability to twist the truth, may be sufficient to convince someone that they did not see what they thought they saw after scrutinizing your disguise.

Prerequisites: Alertness, Deceitful, Persuasive

You may immediately make a DC 20 Sense Motive check as a free action if your disguise fails to convince someone. Success allows for a Bluff check as a standard action at your earliest opportunity (hoping the other person does not act on their suspicions before then.) Apply a penalty to the Bluff check equal to the amount the subject's Perception check defeated your Disguise check by.

So long as the other person does not take action preventing such an outcome before you have the opportunity to make this Bluff check (such as by ripping your disguise off), a successful Bluff will convince the subject that your disguise is genuine—making the subject second guess their initial deduction. Failing the Bluff check has the same result as the disguise failing to begin with.

Using Second Guess to convince someone of the validity of an otherwise failed disguise may only be attempted once per day on the same person, per disguise. Each different disguise allows another attempt for that day on that person should the new disguise also fail to convince the subject.

Shield Rush

Combining your proficiency for charging into battle with your skill with a shield allows you to use the latter to ram your opponents.

Prerequisites: Improved Bull Rush, Improved Shield Bash, Power Attack, Shield Proficiency

You can sacrifice your shield's AC bonus in order to gain a +2 CMB bonus while using the bull rush maneuver and wielding a light shield or a +4 bonus for a heavy shield.

Staggering Blow

You can use your blunted weapon or the flat of your blade to strike a vulernable spot and stagger your foe rather than harm him.

Prerequisites: Bludgeoner φ, Dazing Assault α, Weapon Focus

As a standard action, a slashing or blunt weapon for which you have the Weapon Focus feat may attempt a dazing attack with a -4 penalty to the attack roll against a living opponent wearing light or no armour, and having no natural armor bonus. Weapons intended to only inflict nonlethal damage do not suffer this penalty. If the attack succeeds, the target must pass a (DC 10 + damage) Fortitude saving throw or be considered *staggered* until the end of their next round. Although damage is rolled to determine the Fortitude saving throw's DC, no actual damage is inflicted upon the target.

Steady Step

Extensive expertise at circumventing detrimental terrain and situational conditions makes you better able to deal with them as a matter of course.

Prerequisites: Acrobatic, Acrobatic Steps, Nimble Moves

Conditional DC modifiers for Acrobatics checks are changed to the following:

3. feat synergy

Acrobatics Modifiers	DC Modifier
Slightly obstructed (gravel, sand)	+0
Severely obstructed (cavern, rubble)	+2
Slightly slippery (wet)	+0
Severely slippery (icy)	+3
Slightly sloped (<45°)	+1
Severely sloped (>45°)	+3
Slightly unsteady (boat in rough water)	+1
Moderately unsteady (boat in a storm)	+3
Severely unsteady (earthquake)	+7
Move at full speed on narrow or uneven surfaces	+3 *

* This does not apply to checks made to jump.

Stop Charge

You can stop an opponent's charge with a ranged attack into the right location on him or his mount at just the right moment.

Prerequisites: Deadly Aim, Vital Strike, Weapon Focus

If you have readied an action, you may attempt to interrupt a charging opponent using the ranged attack to which Weapon Focus applies. Make a (DC equal to the target's attack roll) Sense Motive check, or Handle Animal check if targeting a horse or other mounted beast. If successful, you make a ranged attack with a -4 penalty against the charging opponent at any desired point along its charging route. Failure indicates you misread the target's intentions and your attack goes wide, automatically missing and allowing the target to continue charging as normal (and, if you were the charge's target, granting your opponent a +2 damage bonus against you.)

A successful ranged attack against the target forces it to succeed at a (DC 10 + damage suffered) Will saving throw or it will stop at the desired spot along its charging route. If the target is a mount, its riders must also make a (DC 10 + damage suffered) Ride check or be thrown. If the saving throw succeeds, the target suffers the damage from your ranged attack but may continue with its charge as normal.

Sure Grip

Combining your exceptional acrobatics and athletic capabilities results in an improved reaction time and better ability to find a secure handhold while trying to arrest your fall while climbing.

Prerequisites: Acrobatic, Athletic, Skill Focus (Climb)

Climb checks to catch yourself on a wall while falling are (wall's DC + 10) or (slope's DC + 5) to catch yourself while falling down a slope. Also, your Climb check DC, should you succeed at the melee touch attack when attempting to catch a falling character, is (wall's DC + 5.)

Swinging Attack

You may attack an opponent while swinging from a hanging object, such as a chandelier, wall hanging, rope, or vines.

Prerequisites: Athletic, Combat Expertise, Nimble Moves

You may attempt one of three possible effects when you start your turn hanging onto a rope or other hanging object:

1) Initiate a bull rush that will add a +1 circumstance bonus to the Strength check for every 5 feet you move. Unlike a normal bull rush, this does not provoke an attack of opportunity.

2) Gain a +1 circumstance bonus to attack for higher ground while suffering no attack of opportunity for swinging by the defender as you make a melee attack.

3) Make a trip attack with a +1 circumstance bonus to the opposed roll for every 5 feet travelled. The trip attack does not provoke an attack of opportunity and inflicts 1d6 points of nonlethal damage unto the target. If you are tripped during your own trip attempt, you are pulled from the hanging object and take 1d6 points of nonlethal damage, falling 5 feet away from your opponent.

You may attempt a DC 15 Acrobatics check as a free action in order to dismount next to the target while performing any of these effects. Failing the check means you are prone. Instead of dismounting you may also opt to hold onto the hanging object until your next action.

Treasonous Dodge

You twist and maneuver out of the way of two flanking opponents in such a way as to trick them into attacking each other.

Prerequisites: Agile Maneuvers, Dodge, Flanking Foil ᵠ, Mobility, Spring Attack

If you are not flat-footed or otherwise denied your Dodge bonus, and are flanked by two opponents, you may make a single Reflex saving throw against the highest attack roll of the two as a move action. If the saving throw succeeds, the attacks are instead directed at the other attacker who is positioned opposite them. Both attacks strike at you as normal if the saving throw fails, granting both a +2 circumstance bonus to attack and damage.

If you simultaneously attempt this against more than one pair of flanking attackers you suffer a cumulative -2 penalty to your Reflex save per additional pair after the first. In such instances, make one Reflex saving throw for all the attackers but consider the results separately per pair rather than needing to defeat them all as a group.

If the attacker's weapon does not have sufficient reach to attack the other flanking opponent, the attack merely misses instead.

For example, if you are flanked by two opponents who roll a 12 and 15 to attack and your Reflex saving throw results in a 16, one attacker's strike is directed at his ally with a roll of 12 while he is himself attacked by his ally with an attack roll of 15. If you are later flanked by three pairs of opponents from different directions with attack rolls of 13 and 13, 17 and 9, and 16 and 14, a single Reflex saving throw is rolled with a -4 penalty. A result of 16 means the first and third pairs of flanking opponents are tricked into attacking each other, but the second pair (the 17 and 9 attack rolls) still manage to attack you wile gaining the +2 bonus to do so resulting from your failure.

Vault Opponent

You are able to leap over your opponent during combat, landing beside or behind him.

Prerequisites: Acrobatic, Agile Maneuvers, Sidestep ᵃ, Step Up

A successful DC 25 Acrobatics check allows you to flip over an adjacent opponent who is no more than one size category larger than you in place of your usual 5-foot step. This elicits an attack of opportunity unless you also succeed at a DC 20 Reflex saving throw. Failing the Acrobatics check means you fall prone where you are. You cannot otherwise use a move action that round, although any full-round action is allowed.

If successfully completed, this surprise move leaves that opponent flat-footed against you for the rest of the round. You may use Vault Opponent against that same foe more than once in a single encounter, but subsequent successes does not inflict flat-footed status because the maneuver is no longer as surprising.

Whirling Deflection

Your superior reflexes allow the opportunity to deflect more than one ranged attack sent in your direction.

Prerequisites: Combat Reflexes, Deflect Arrows, Improved Unarmed Strike, Lightning Reflexes

You may deflect an additional amount of ranged weapon attacks as is equal to your Dexterity bonus. The limitations listed under Deflect Arrows otherwise still apply but any deflection attempts beyond the first (automatically successful) deflection requires its own Reflex saving throws with a DC equal to that attack's roll. Each deflection attempt beyond the second incurs a cumulative DC +2 modifier. A successful Reflex saving throw means the attack was deflected.

Make the Reflex saving throw in the order the attack rolls were made, meaning you cannot decide which attacks will be deflected first. Furthermore, if you fail a Reflex saving throw against a particular ranged attack you cannot use one of your other remaining attempts to try again.

Each ranged attack beyond the automatically successful first deflected attack reduces your amount of attacks of opportunity for that round via the Combat Reflexes feat by 1.

For example, a character with a Dexterity bonus of +3 is targeted by five ranged attacks with rolls to hit of 20, 18, 14, 16, and 20. The first attack (20) is automatically successful, as covered by Deflect Arrows. The second attack (18) requires a DC 18 Reflex save to deflect, the third attack (14) requires a DC 16 Reflex save (14 + 2), the fourth attack (16) requires a DC 20 Reflex save (16 + 2 + 2), and the fifth attack cannot be deflected because the character is limited to a maximum of three additional deflection attempts by his +3 Dexterity bonus.

Whirling Return

Now you are able to use more than just one of your enemies' ranged attacks against themselves!

Prerequisites: Combat Reflexes, Deflect Arrows, Improved Unarmed Strike, Lightning Reflexes, Snatch Arrows

This Synergy Effect is much the same as Whirling Deflection except it allows multiple weapons to be thrown back or kept for later instead of merely being deflected. Each thrown weapon beyond the first that is thrown back suffers a cumulative −4 penalty to attack.

You may not make more additional Whirling Return attacks using caught thrown weapons than your Dexterity bonus or the normal amount of attacks you may make during a full-attack action, whichever is lower.

Whistling Shot

There is a chance you will hear the whistling of an arrow fired your way (or whatever sound is appropriate to the ranged attack) and be able to fully defend against it despite the attacker being invisible or taking you by surprise.

Prerequisites: Alertness, Blind-Fight, Improved Blind-Fight[a]

You may attempt a Perception check against a ranged attack from an invisible or otherwise undetected opponent as a reaction, using the normal sound-based Perception DC of the attack, +5. Any attack bonus for being invisible or hidden is negated if the Perception check succeeds.

This Synergy Effect is not possible in silenced areas or against ranged attacks that are completely and truly silent.

Chapter 4

Class Synergy

A character's choice of classes is perhaps the most significant contributor to how it will develop in terms of the game's mechanics, and this is especially true of multiclassed characters that mix abilities from different classes in a way that is intended to compliment the whole. However, even though there is a degree of abilities that complement each other regarding the standard process of multiclassing, the potential for even greater relationships between classes in such a scenario exists, its potential untapped. This is where Class Synergy enters the picture.

The purpose of multiclassing is to create a character that can draw upon the abilities of different—and often very disparate—foci, be they spiritual, martial, arcane, or otherwise, in such a way as to make the whole stronger by means of this diversity. Beyond this resulting ability variation, however, the game does not account for any interaction between abilities of different classes despite someone learning components of what are essentially different specialties even though it is reasonable to conclude that the opposite should be true: a multiclassed character should naturally find ways to unite these abilities in a manner representing this combined knowledge. And this is exactly what Class Synergy does.

By not presuming a multiclassed character is not merely a collection of piecemeal abilities intended to

Terms of Class Synergy

Prerequisites: The class abilities required to work together in order to obtain the desired Class Synergy Effect. The amount of classes associated with these abilities may grow as new rulebooks, including third-party products, are released and new classes become available.

Synergy Effect: The desired benefit obtained by using the specified class abilities together.

Class Synergy and Game Balance

Because the standard game mechanics were not designed with the intent of having class abilities interact in a manner introduced by Class Synergy, utilizing them may upset game balance in some instances. If Gamemasters feel this is the case, a simple way of approaching the matter is requiring each Class Synergy Effect to be selected as a feat of the same name. Alternatively, it may be purchased as a class ability, such as a rage power, form of bardic performance, or rogue talent, if a class related to one of the Class Synergy Effect's prerequisites allows for selecting such abilities.

stand on their own, the concept of Class Synergy instead assumes such a character would find a way to get these abilities to work together in new ways that were not intended—or even possible—on their own. Whether by experimentation, study, or innate capability, a multiclassed character is able to get more out of the standard class abilities than can a single classed character by combining what he knows of each. In this way, Class Synergy is perhaps the natural and thus-far unexplored conclusion to be drawn from the concept of multiclassing.

Classy Synergy Effects primarily focus on the abilities of base and core classes rather than prestige classes. The reasoning for this is simple: one of the principal design tenets of creating a prestige class is to build its abilities upon the foundation of a core or base class. As such, its seems somewhat redundant, both from a design perspective and one of practicality, to unbalance this design principle by adding a layer of synergy effects atop it.

Classy Synergy Effects are lost if the character is denied, permanently or temporarily, any of the class abilities counted among its prerequisites.

4. Class Synergy

Class Synergy Effects

Name	Prerequisites	Synergy Effect
Agile Stride	*Trackless step*, *travel domain*, *woodland stride*	Gain your *trackless step* and *woodland stride* benefits while using *agile step*, regardless of the terrain
Ambush Strike	*Favored terrain*, *sneak attack*	Prepare an area of favored terrain to gain a Stealth and attack bonus against a surprised opponent
Arcane Alchemy	*Alchemy*[α], arcane spells	You may attempt a Craft (alchemy) check to translate arcane spells into alchemical potions
Arcane Blooded	*Arcane bloodline*, *magic domain*	Use similar but not identical divine spells as counterspells versus arcane magic
Ballad of Ire	*Bardic performance: dirge of doom*, *favored enemy*, *rage*	+2 critical threat range against your favored enemy while raging at the cost of a -2 penalty to skills and being fatigued longer
Bardic Blood	*Bardic performamcne*, *maestro bloodline*[μ]	You can use your *bardic performance* for a number of rounds per day equal to 8 + your Charisma modifier.
Beast Walker	*Animal domain*, *wild shape*	*Wild shape* requires a swift action to use
Blessed Arcana	Arcane spells, *magic domain*	You may swap Knowledge (arcana) and Knowledge (religion) for the other skill's checks
Blessed Fury	*Chaos domain*, *rage*, and *battle mystery*[α] or *war domain*	If you kill an opponent while raging you are allowed a Fortitude saving throw to resist becoming *fatigued* when the *rage* ends
Bushwhack	*Dead shot deed*[φ], *sneak attack*, *targeting deed*[φ]	A *sneak attack* coupled with *dead shot* or *targeting* increases the former's damage die from 1d6 to 1d10, but with consequences
Challenge of Hatred	*Challenge*[α][φ], and *smite evil* or *smite good*[α] or *favored enemy*	A successful Will saving throw means not using a daily *challenge* allotment when challenging an appropriate enemy
Channel Rage	*Channel energy*, *rage*	Spend *rage* to gain an additional use of *channel energy*
Chaos Blooded	*Chaos domain*, *aberrant bloodline*	Targets of chaos domain spells are -2 to saving throws
Cruel Performance	*Bardic performance*, *cruelty*[α], *touch of corruption*[α]	Your *bardic performance* carries your wounding effects to anyone nearby
Damned Companion	*Touch of corruption*[α], and an animal/creature companion class ability	Your companion may use your *touch of corruption* ability
Dance of Fists	*Bardic performance*, *flurry of blows*	Replace *flurry of blows* attack rolls with a Perform (dance) check
Dancing Roll	*Versatile performance*, *defensive roll*	Replace the Reflex save of a *defensive roll* with a Perform (dance) check
Divine Companion	Divine spells, and a class ability that creates a close bond to an animal, object, or creature	Your companion may substitute for your divine focus
Divine Knowledge	*Knowledge domain* or *lore mystery*[α], *bardic knowledge* or *lore*	You may re-roll one Knowledge check per game session
Evil's Select	*Evil domain*, *smite good*[α]	Your ability to *smite good* may also cause the target to become *staggered*
Favored Commander	*Inspiring command*[α], and *battle mystery*[α] or *war domain*	Add your Wisdom bonus to your Leadership score
Favored Monster	*Favored enemy*, *monster lore*[α]	You may try again on a failed Knowledge check for your *favored enemy* at DC +5

Class Synergy Effects, continued

Name	Prerequisites	Synergy Effect
Favored Stride	*Favored terrain, trackless step, woodland stride*	Benefit from *trackless step* and *woodland stride* in *favored terrain*
Flame Blooded	*Fire domain* or *flame mystery* [α], and *fire elemental bloodline*	You are +2 to save versus fire subtype spells
Furious Smite Evil	*Rage, smite evil*	Use *rage* in order to *smite evil*
Furious Smite Good	*Rage, smite good* [α]	Use *rage* in order to *smite good*
Good's Select	*Good domain, smite evil*	Your ability to *smite evil* may also cause the target to become *staggered*
Grotesque Beast	*Mutagen* [α], *wild shape*	Your beast form takes on more monstrous qualities
Hallowed Terrain	*Terrain mastery* [α], *travel domain*	+5 feet to movement within a favored terrain
Holy Companion	*Lay on hands*, and an animal/creature companion class ability	Your companion may use your *lay on hands* ability
Honorable Defense	*Defensive stance* [α], *honorable stand* [φ]	*Defensive stance* uses half the normal amount of rounds while also making an *honorable stand*
Hymnal Channeling	*Bardic performance, channel energy*	Use your voice as a divine focus to *channel energy*, potentially expanding the burst radius by doing so
Liquid Rage	*Alchemy* [α], *mutagen* [α], *rage*	Create a mutagen that regains or extends your *rage* by 2d4 rounds
Merciful Performance	*Bardic performance, lay on hands, mercy*	Your *bardic performance* carries your healing effects to anyone nearby
Performing Companion	*Bardic performance*, an animal/creature companion class ability	Your companion may employ your *bardic performance* ability
Quivering Performance	*Bardic performance, quivering palm*	You may use your *bardic performance* to use *quivering palm* on multiple targets, but at reduced potency
Raging Companion	*Rage*, an animal/creature companion class ability	Your companion may employ your *rage* ability
Raging Performance	*Bardic performance, rage*	Gain a +4 Perform bonus or +2 DC bonus to your *bardic performance* if you make your *rage* a part of the performance
Raging Spell	*Arcane spells, rage*	Use *rage* to cast an arcane spell without expending a spell slot
Sacred Deception	Any *advanced rogue talent, trickery domain*	Gain a +2 bonus to a single Bluff, Disable Device, Disguise, or Sleight of Hand check
Sacred Shield	*Defensive stance* [α], *protection domain*	You retain your shield's AC bonus while flat-footed.

Agile Stride

With an expression of your power, you step nimbly and without sign across the rough ground, leaving your pursuers behind.

Prerequisites: *Trackless step* (druid), *travel domain* (cleric, inquisitor [α]), *woodland stride* (druid)

When using the *agile feet* ability of the *travel domain*, you may apply the benefits of both the *trackless step* and *woodland stride* abilities, even if the terrain being moved through does not normally apply to the latter two abilities.

Ambush Strike

Such is your stealth and mastery of terrain that you may strike from hiding within familiar ground.

Prerequisites: *Favored terrain* (horizon walker [α], nature warden [α], ranger), *sneak attack* (arcane trickster, assassin, master spy [α], ninja [φ], rogue)

By taking 1d6+4 minutes to prepare up to an acre of your *favored terrain* before a battle and then conceal yourself within it, you gain a +10 competence bonus to

Class Synergy Effects, continued

Name	Prerequisites	Synergy Effect
Safe Terrain	*Evasion, favored terrain, trap sense*	Add your *favored terrain* bonus to your *trap sense* benefits regarding traps encountered in the appropriate favored terrain
Shadow-Shrouded	*Darkeness domain*, and *shadow illusion* or *shadow bloodline*[α]	Lighting conditions regarding you are considered one degree darker than is normal for the environment
Showboat	*Bardic performance*, any *deeds*[φ]	You can start a *bardic performance* as a free action while using a gunslinger *deeds*
Sneaky Companion	*Rogue talent* or *ninja trick*[φ], and an animal/creature companion class ability	Your companion gains new class skills and may replace some of its abilities with those of its master
Stone Blooded	*Earth domain* or *stone mystery*[α], and *deep earth*[α] or *earth elemental bloodline*	You have the tremorsense ability
Stunning Performance	*Bardic performance, ki pool, stunning fist* (requires the ability, not the feat)	Your bardic performance can inflict your *stunning fist* effect to anyone in range who can perceive your performance
Tomb Blooded	*Bones mystery*[α] or *death domain*, and *undead bloodline*	You are +2 to save versus Necromancy
Track Evil	*Detect evil, track*; these must be class abilities and not spells	Make a Perception check to increase your chances of tracking evil prey
Track Good	*Detect good*[α], *track*; these must be class abilities and not spells	Make a Perception check to increase your chances of tracking good prey
Vendure Blooded	*Nature mystery*[α] or *plant domain*, and *verdant bloodline*[α]	You gain a +2 bonus to Fortitude and Will saving throws versus many plant-based effects
Vitae Blooded	*Glory domain* or *life mystery*[α], and *undead bloodline*	You gain a +2 bonus to resist undead abilities and death spells
Water Blooded	*Water domain* or *wave mystery*[α], and *aquatic*[α] or *water elemental bloodline*	You can hold your breath three times longer than normal in water
Wind Blooded	*Air domain* or *wind mystery*[α], and *air elemental bloodline*	You are +2 to Fly skill checks

[α] See the *Pathfinder® Roleplaying Game: Advanced Player's Guide*™

[μ] See the *Pathfinder® Roleplaying Game: Ultimate Magic*™

[φ] See the *Pathfinder® Roleplaying Game: Ultimate Combat*™

Stealth checks and are +5 to attack rolls against surprised opponents within the first round of a combat occurring within that area.

Once you have revealed yourself and engaged in combat you must prepare the area and hide yet again in order to regain these benefits.

Arcane Alchemy

Your alchemical ingenuity has shown you the way to distill your wizardry into a liquid surprise you shall reserve for the next opponent you face.

Prerequisites: *Alchemy* (alchemist[α]), arcane spells

You can brew potions of any arcane spell you know (up to 3rd level), using your alchemist level as your caster level. The spell must be one that normally can be made into a potion. Such potions cost twice the normal amount and require a (DC 10 + price / 2, rounded down) Craft (alchemy) skill check. Failure means the potion does not work and its ingredients are wasted and unusable.

Arcane Blooded

The magic that runs through your blood and the divine favor you enjoy allows you to transmute divine magic to counter the arcane.

Prerequisites: *Arcane bloodline* (sorcerer), *magic domain* (cleric, inquisitor[α])

If you succeed at a Spellcraft check to counterspell, you may use a similar divine spell of equal or greater level to counter an arcane spell instead of casting an identical arcane spell, as normal. It is up to the Gamemaster's discretion as to what divine spell is sufficiently similar to act as a substitute in this manner. For example, the Gamemaster may decide that *flame strike* can act as a counterspell to a *fireball*.

Ballad of Ire

You work yourself into a deeper rage by fueling your own emotions with a song of blood, glory, and vengeance against your hated enemy.

Prerequisites: *Bardic performance: dirge of doom* (bard), *favored enemy* (ranger), *rage* (barbarian)

Your enhanced fury grants you a +2 morale bonus to all weapon critical threat ranges against your favored enemy while raging, but imposes a -2 penalty to all skill checks and extends the duration of fatigue following the rage to triple rather than double the time spent raging.

Bardic Blood

The music that runs through your veins makes your bardic talents more enduring.

Prerequisites: *Bardic perforamcne* (bard), *maestro bloodline* (sorcerer)[μ]

You can use your *bardic performance* for a number of rounds per day equal to 8 + your Charisma modifier.

Beast Walker

Your divine favor and divine attunement allows you to more easily shift into bestial form.

Prerequisites: *Animal domain* (cleric, inquisitor [α]), *wild shape* (druid)

Changing in or out of your *wild shape* requires a swift action rather than standard action.

Blessed Arcana

To you, matters of faith and arcana are virtually interchangeable.

Prerequisites: Arcane spells, *magic domain* (cleric, inquisitor [α])

You may substitute your Knowledge (religion) for Knowledge (arcana) checks, and vice versa, but do not add your Int modifier when doing so.

Blessed Fury

Your god favors giving oneself to battle and so may spare you its exhausting toll if you offer up sufficient sacrifices with your fury.

Prerequisites: *Chaos domain* (cleric, inquisitor [α]), *rage* (barbarian), and *battle mystery* (oracle) [α] or *war domain* (cleric, inquisitor [α])

If you slay an opponent in your *rage*, when it ends you are allowed a DC 20 Fortitude saving throw that, if successful, will prevent you from suffering the usual fatigue. You gain a +1 sacred or profane (as appropriate) bonus to this saving throw for every opponent after the first that you killed while raging.

Bushwhack

Carefully stalking your foe, you draw a bead on him with your pistol and pull the trigger, striking him from concealment with deadly effect.

Prerequisites: *Dead shot deed* (gunslinger) [φ], *sneak attack* (arcane trickster, assassin, master spy [α], ninja, rogue), *targeting deed* (gunslinger) [φ]

When making a *sneak attack* simultaneously with either the *dead shot deed* or *targeting deed*, you roll 1d10 instead of the usual 1d6 per die of damage your *sneak attack* normally inflicts.

Using Bushwhack against someone is seen as a cowardly act, however, and thus costs 1 additional grit point. What's more, for the rest of the encounter you do not regain any grit no matter what actions you take.

You cannot deal nonlethal damage with your *sneak attack* with Bushwack.

Challenge of Hatred

Your enemy stands before you, your loathing palpable. You raise your blade to your brow in both salute and challenge before stepping forward to rid the world of such a despised foe.

Prerequisites: *Challenge* (cavalier [α], samurai [φ]), and *smite evil* (paladin) or *smite good* (antipaladin [α]) or *favored enemy* (ranger)

When you *challenge* an opponent who is evil (paladin), good (antipaladin), or a favored enemy (ranger), respectively, a daily *challenge* is not expended if you succeed at a (DC 10 + challenged opponent's HD) Will saving throw.

You cannot use Challenge of Hatred in two consecutive rounds.

4. Class Synergy

Channel Rage

You tap into your rage, channeling and unleashing divine energy.

Prerequisites: *Channel energy* (antipaladin[a], cleric, paladin), *rage* (barbarian)

By expending one round of your *rage* ability's daily allotment, you can use *channel energy* an additional time that day. You are *fatigued* for a minimum of two rounds afterward, however, as though you used *rage*.

Chaos Blooded

The divine touch of chaos is fueled by your tainted bloodline.

Prerequisites: *Chaos domain* (cleric, inquisitor [a]), *aberrant bloodline* (sorcerer)

Targets of any divine chaos domain spell you cast suffer a -2 penalty to their saving throws.

Cruel Performance

Your chant of darkness and evil spreads among your enemies, opening horrible wounds upon their flesh.

Prerequisites: *Bardic performance* (bard), *cruelty* (antipaladin)[a], *touch of corruption* (antipaladin)[a]

By undertaking a *bardic performance* that expresses the devotion of your dark faith, you may spread the effects of your *touch of corruption* ability and any applied *cruelty*, to anyone in a 30-foot burst of you. This requires a DC 20 Perform check and affects everyone other than yourself, regardless of allegiance. A target may resist, if desired, by making a Will saving throw against a DC equal to your Perform check's result.

Cruel Performance uses both one round's worth of *bardic performance* and one daily use of *touch of corruption*.

Damned Companion

The dark divinity that has made you one of its champions has extended some benefits of its darkness to your bonded companion.

Prerequisites: *Touch of corruption* (antipaladin) [a], and a class ability that creates a close bond to an animal or creature, such as the familiar provided by Arcane Bond or animal companion from Nature Bond

The unholy power that works through you can be channeled through the bond you share with your companion, allowing it to employ your *touch of corruption* and *cruelty* abilities. Doing so expends one of your daily *touch of corruption* uses, however.

Dance of Fists

You flow about with a dancer's grace, striking out with fist and foot as though your attacks were part of a grand choreography.

Prerequisites: *Bardic performance* (bard), *flurry of blows* (monk)

You may substitute a Perform (dance) skill check for your attack roll when using *flurry of blows*. Your attacks suffer the following penalties when doing so instead of the usual *flurry of blows* attack modifiers: -1 to the first and second, -4 to the third and fourth, -8 to the fifth and sixth, and -12 to the seventh attacks.

Dance of Fists uses one round's worth of *bardic performance*.

Dancing Roll

You are so light on your feet that you are able to dance out of harm's way.

Prerequisites: *Versatile performance: dance* (bard), *defensive roll* (rogue)

Replace your Reflex saving throw roll with a Peform (dance) check with regards to using *defensive roll*, with the same results as normal for success or failure.

Divine Companion

Such is your relationship with your bonded companion that the divine power you serve has recognized it and anointed it with its blessings, allowing its intent to be worked through the companion.

Prerequisites: Divine spells, and a class ability that creates a close bond to an animal, object, or creature, such as the familiar provided by Arcane Bond or animal companion from Nature Bond

Your companion, be it creature, beast, or object, may take the place of a required divine focus while casting divine spells, using the *channel energy* ability, or for any other process that requires the use of a divine focus. This substitution is automatic if you are in physical contact with your companion, but requires a (DC 10 + 1 per foot of distance away) Charisma check if not.

Divine Knowledge

Knowledge passed down through your connection to the divine may, at times, correct information as you personally understand it to be.

Prerequisites: *Knowledge domain* (cleric, inquisitor ᵃ) or *lore mystery* (oracle) ᵃ, *bardic knowledge* (bard) or *lore* (loremaster)

You may re-roll any Knowledge check once per game session. You must abide by this re-roll's result, even if it is unsuccessful.

Evil's Select

Your divine patron recognizes your extraordinary dedication to all that is evil by increasing the potency of your ability to smite good.

Prerequisites: *Evil domain* (cleric, inquisitor ᵃ), *smite good* (antipaladin) ᵃ

A target of *smite good* who suffers damage from the assault must also succeed at a (DC 10 + smite damage) Will saving throw or be *staggered*.

Favored Commander

Divine favor flows through you, affecting your ability to lead and command.

Prerequisites: *Inspiring command* (battle herald) ᵃ, and *battle mystery* (oracle) ᵃ or *war domain* (cleric, inquisitor ᵃ)

In addition to the usual elements that contribute to your Leadership score, add your Wisdom bonus.

Favored Monster

Your intimate familiarity with the enemy grants you a better chance of sneaking past its defenses.

Prerequisites: *Favored enemy* (ranger), *monster lore* (inquisitor) ᵃ

If you fail a Knowledge check regarding a *favored enemy* you may try again by dredging the depths of your knowledge, but doing so increases the previous DC by 5.

Favored Stride

As though it were the depths of nature's greenest wilds, your familiarity with the land allows you to move through it with unsurpassed ease and stealth

Prerequisites: *Favored terrain* (ranger), *trackless step* (druid), *woodland stride* (druid)

While in a favored terrain, you may apply the benefits of both the *trackless step* and *woodland stride* abilities, even if the terrain being moved through does not normally apply to the latter two abilities.

Flame Blooded

Your life's blood burns with elemental power, allowing the divine purchase with which to protect you.

Prerequisites: *Fire domain* (cleric, inquisitor ᵃ) or *flame mystery* (oracle) ᵃ, and *fire elemental bloodline* (sorcerer)

You gain a +2 sacred or profane (as appropriate) bonus to saving throws versus spells of the fire subtype.

Furious Smite Evil

You are able to discharge your rage in favor of your holy cause, allowing it to fuel your assaults against evil.

Prerequisites: *Rage* (barbarian), *smite evil* (paladin)

Succeeding at (DC 5 + paladin level) Charisma check allows you to expend *rage* in order to instead *smite evil*, allowing a paladin to employ the latter more times per day than is usual per round of *rage* so spent. Failing this check still uses up one round's worth of *rage*. You are *fatigued* as though ending a *rage* once the Furious Smite is over.

4. CLASS SYNERGY

Furious Smite Good

You are able to discharge your rage in favor of your unholy cause, allowing it to fuel your assaults against good.

Prerequisites: *Rage* (barbarian), *smite good* (antipaladin)[a]

Succeeding at (DC 5 + antipaladin level) Charisma check allows you to expend *rage* in order to instead *smite good*, allowing an antipaladin to employ the latter more times per day than is usual per round of *rage* so spent. Failing this check still uses up one round's worth of *rage*. You are *fatigued* as though ending a *rage* once the Furious Smite is over.

Good's Select

Your divine patron recognizes your extraordinary dedication to championing good by increasing the potency of your ability to smite evil.

Prerequisites: *Good domain* (cleric, inquisitor [a]), *smite evil* (paladin)

A target of *smite evil* who suffers damage from the assault must also succeed at a (DC 10 + smite damage) Will saving throw or be *staggered*.

Grotesque Beast

Rushing through your assumed shape, you can feel the mutagen making you something more than just a beast.

Prerequisites: *Mutagen* (alchemist)[a], *wild shape* (druid)

Combining the influence of a *mutagen* while using *wild shape* results in a monstrous appearing parody of the desired animal form. This increases the *mutagen's* natural armor bonus from +2 to +4, but also adds a -4 Charisma penalty, in addition to any other penalty the *mutagen* causes.

Hallowed Terrain

The lands you favor are blessed by the Divine through your presence there, allowing you swifter travel.

Prerequisites: *Terrain mastery* (horizon walker), *travel domain* (cleric, inquisitor[a])

You increase all forms of movement by +5 feet while in a *favored terrain*.

Holy Companion

The divine power that has made you one of its champions has extended some benefits of its grace to your bonded companion.

Prerequisites: *Lay on hands* (paladin), and a class ability that creates a close bond to an animal or creature, such as the familiar provided by Arcane Bond or animal companion from Nature Bond

The holy power that works through you can be channeled through the bond you share with your companion, allowing it to employ your *lay on hands* and *mercy* abilities. Doing so expends one of your daily *lay on hands* uses, however.

Honorable Defense

You rconcentration firm, you dig in and ready yourself to withstand the coming tide of enemies—until death if need be.

Prerequisites: *Defensive stance* (stalwart defender) [a], *honorable stand* (samurai)[φ]

Every two rounds of using *defensive stance* while making an *honorable stand* only uses one round of the former ability's daily allotment of total available rounds.

Hymnal Channeling

Your voice becomes the focus of your divine energies.

Prerequisites: *Bardic performance* (bard), *channel energy* (cleric, holy vindicator[α], paladin)

Instead of using a divine focus, you may sing praise to your faith as a hymn, allowing the power of your voice to employ your *channel energy* ability instead. Doing so requires making a Perform (sing) check against a DC equal to your *channel energy* saving throw DC. Success causes your *channel energy* ability to operate in a 30-foot burst around you, as normal, but it will only affect targets who may be influenced by audible components.

Increase the burst range by an additional 30 feet for every point your Perform (sing) check surpasses the DC, but also reduce the saving throw DC against the channeled energy by a cumulative -2 per additional 30 feet band the subject is in. Feats, magic items, or other abilities that increase or reduce the channel energy abilitie's normal burst radius of 30 feet similarly influences this Class Synergy Effect.

For example, a Perform (sing) roll of 18 versus a DC of 16 would mean the burst would be 90 feet, but creatures between 31 and 60 feet would save against DC 14 and those between 61 and 90 feet would save against DC 12.

Hymnal Channeling uses both one round's worth of *bardic performance* and one daily use of *channel energy*.

Liquid Rage

As the liquid concoction burns its way down your throat, you feel the rage within your heart similarly start to burn anew.

Prerequisites: *Alchemy* (alchemist) [α], *mutagen* (alchemist) [α], *rage* (barbarian)

You may create a mutagen that allows your body to better withstand your *rage*, restoring 2d4 rounds worth of expended *rage*, up to your daily maximum. It can also extend a current rage by the same amount of time. The usal restrictions and rules for mutagens otherwise apply.

Merciful Performance

As you sing about the love your god has for its devotees, you see the wounds on your nearby allies begin to close.

Prerequisites: *Bardic performance* (bard), *lay on hands* (paladin), *mercy* (paladin)

By undertaking a *bardic performance* that expresses the devotion of your faith, you may spread the benefits of your *lay on hands* ability, as well as any applied *mercy*, to anyone in a 30-foot burst of you. This requires a DC 20 Perform check. This affects everyone except yourself, regardless of allegiance. A target may resist, if desired, by making a Will saving throw against a DC equal to your Perform check's result.

Merciful Performance uses both one round's worth of *bardic performance* and one daily use of *lay on hands*.

Performing Companion

Your companion is able to draw upon your talent in order to undertake a bardic performance of its own.

Prerequisites: *Bardic performance* (bard), and a class ability that creates a close bond to an animal or creature, such as the familiar provided by Arcane Bond or animal companion from Nature Bond

Whether by drawing upon the bond between the two of you, having learned how to by spending so much time around you, or via some other appropriate means, your companion is able to make use of your *bardic performance* ability. A companion without a Perform skill of its own uses your Perform skill but at half the ranks while doing so. Use the instance with the most ranks if you have multiple appropriate Perform skills. Subtract the amount of rounds the companion spends using *bardic performance* from your daily allotment. You and your companion may use *bardic performance* simultaneously and need not employ the same type of performance.

Quivering Performance

As you sing, you send deadly vibrations through the air into the foes gathering around you in preparation for your deadly strikes

Prerequisites: *Bardic performance* (bard), *quivering palm* (monk)

Your *quivering palm* ability may instead be passed through vibrations in the air using a *bardic performance* involving audible components. Every desired target (you may choose) within range of the *bardic performance* must make a Fortitude saving throw to resist its influence. Unlike a normal *quivering palm*, a Quivering Performance does not add your Wis modifier to the save DC. The duration of the effect before it expires is counted in hours instead of days, as usual.

4. CLASS SYNERGY

Quivering Performance uses both one round's worth of *bardic performance* and the daily use of *quivering palm*.

Raging Companion

You may pass your feral rage along to your companion through the preternatural bond that ties the two of you together.

Prerequisites: *Rage* (barbarian), and a class ability that creates a close bond to an animal or creature, such as the familiar provided by Arcane Bond or animal companion from Nature Bond

You can make your animal companion, familiar, eidolon, or whatever enter a rage, as per your *rage* class ability (including any *rage powers*, if possible), granting it all the results you would normally acquire from the ability. Your companion's *rage* uses rounds from your daily allotment.

If desired, the companion may resist you imposing your rage upon it by succeeding at a (DC 10 + Charisma modifier) Will saving throw.

Raging Performance

You harness your rage and use it in your performance, giving it a depth of emotional reality that is otherwise difficult to achieve.

Prerequisites: *Bardic performance* (bard), *rage* (barbarian)

Using your *rage* ability at the same time as *bardic performance* grants a +4 bonus to the latter's Perform check or a +2 bonus to its DC, as appropriate. You do not gain any of the usual rage bonuse, however. Such a Raging Performance is limited in duration to the amount of available rounds left that day for the *rage* ability and does not use any of your daily allotment of rounds for *bardic performance*. When the *rage* duration ends, so too does the *bardic performance*. You suffer the usual fatigue that follows a *rage* when the Raging Performance ends.

Raging Spell

You call upon your rage to fuel your arcane spells, drawing upon the energy your fury releases and converting it into magic.

Prerequisites: Arcane spells, *rage* (barbarian)

Instead of expending one of your daily spell slots to cast an arcane spell, you may sacrifice one round's worth of *rage* and make a (DC 10 + spell level) attribute check. The attribute utilized matches that which is relevant to your arcane spellcasting ability—Intelligence for wizards or Charisma for sorcerers, for example. Success allows you to cast a spell you currently otherwise have the ability to cast but doing so does not expend a spell slot. Failing this check means the spell is cast, using its spell slot normally, and the *rage* is also expended.

A Raging Spell causes you to be *fatigued* as though ending a *rage* regardless of whether the attribute check fails or succeeds.

Sacred Deception

Attempting to fool others in pursuit of your thieving ways may draw divine favor.

Prerequisites: Any *advanced rogue talent* (rogue), *trickery domain* (cleric, inquisitor [a])

Gain a +2 sacred or profane (as appropriate) bonus to a single Bluff, Disable Device, Disguise, or Sleight of Hand check. You can only use Sacred Deception once per game session, regardless of what the bonus is applied to.

Sacred Shield

The Powers-from-on-High guide your shield to be where it needs to be when you are caught by surprised.

Prerequisites: *Defensive stance* (stalwart defender)[α], *protection domain* (cleric, inquisitor[α])

You retain your shield's AC bonus while flat-footed if you are in good standing with the divine power you worship.

Safe Terrain

You are so familiar with your favored terrain that you may instinctively sense when someone has trapped it.

Prerequisites: *Evasion* (druid, gunslinger[φ], master chymist[α], monk, ninja[φ], ranger, rogue), *favored terrain* (ranger), *trap sense* (barbarian, rogue)

You add your +2 *favored terrain* bonus to your *trap sense* Reflex saving throw and AC bonuses with regards to encountering traps in your *favored terrain*.

Shadow-Shrouded

Divine shadows reach about and cling to you.

Prerequisites: *Darkness domain* (cleric, inquisitor[α]), and *shadow illusion* (shadowdancer) or *shadow bloodline* (sorcerer)[α]

Shadows surround you, considering you to be in one degree of lighting darker than that of the environment you are in so long as you are in good standing with the divine power you worship. If you are in an area of normal lighting you are considered to be in an area of dim light, for example.

Showboat

Twirling your pistols in ever-widening circles about your body, your opponents stop what they are doing, fascinated by your gunplay even as you quickly press one of the hot pistol barrels against the wound in your thigh, sealing it.

Prerequisites: *Bardic performance* (bard), any *deeds* (gunslinger)[φ]

As a free action, you may activate a *bardic performance* simultaneously while using a *deed* by replacing the former's usual Perform skill check with a Perform (gunplay) check. This only works for a *bardic performance* with a visual component.

Perform (gunplay)

Perform (gunplay) involves using rapid hand movements, tossing the weapon in the air, and so on as a means of entertaining an audience.

Showboat uses both one round's worth of *bardic performance* and the *deed's* grit cost.

Sneaky Companion

While you distract your opponent, your owl silently glides up behind him, using surprise to rake the back of your foe's neck.

Prerequisites: *Rogue talent* (rogue) or *ninja trick* (ninja)[φ], and a class ability that creates a close bond to an animal or creature, such as the familiar provided by Arcane Bond or animal companion from Nature Bond

Your animal companion gain Disable Device (Dex) and Sleight of Hand (Dex) as class skills, and may replace any special abilities it gains from its bond with its master with the *trap sense* (rogue) or *no trace* (ninja) ability, or any *ninja trick* (normal or master) or *rogue talent* (normal or advanced) you know, and/or *sneak attack* abilities.

For example, a multi-classed wizard 4/rogue 1 with a wizard's familiar could replace any of the familiar's alertness, improved envasion, share spells, empathic link, or deliver touch spells special abilities with abilities allowed by Sneaky Companion.

Stone Blooded

Divine energies of the earth resonate through the stone running through your bloods, vibrating into your senses.

Prerequisites: *Earth domain* (cleric, inquisitor[α]) or *stone mystery* (oracle)[α], and *deep earth*[α] or *earth elemental bloodline* (sorcerer)

You acquire tremorsense as a supernatural ability.

Stunning Performance

As you play your instrument, waves of ki energy emenate through the air, stunning your audience in place.

Prerequisites: *Bardic performance* (bard), *ki pool* (monk, ninja[φ]), *stunning fist* (monk; requires the class ability, not the feat)

4. CLASS SYNERGY

Your bardic performance potentially affects anyone who can perceive your performance and is within 30 feet, including allies, requiring a (DC 10 + 1/2 bard level + Cha modifier) Will saving throw. Failure results in the target being affected as per the desired *stunning fist* effect. Use a Will saving throw regardless of the selected *stunning fist* affect.

Stunning Perforamce uses both one round's worth of *bardic performance* and one point from the *ki pool*.

Tomb Blooded

The divine powers that exist beyond the pale veil interacts with the undead taint within your blood, allowing you to better resist necromantic energies.

Prerequisites: *Bones mystery* (oracle) ᵃ or *death domain* (cleric, inquisitorᵃ), and *undead bloodline* (sorcerer)

You gain a +2 sacred or profane (as appropriate) bonus to saving throws versus necromancy spells.

Track Evil

Your ability to sense your prey's evil permits you to follow them more easily.

Prerequisites: *Detect evil* (paladin), *track* (ranger, inquisitor ᵃ); these must be class abilities and not spells

Making a successful Perception check against the tracking Survival check's DC as a move action allows you to add a sacred bonus to your Survival check to track someone or something of an evil alignment. This bonus is +2 if your prey is neutral evil, +5 if lawful evil, and +8 if chaotic evil.

Track Good

Your ability to sense your prey's goodness permits you to follow them more easily.

Prerequisites: *Detect good* (antipaladin) ᵃ, *track* (ranger, inquisitor ᵃ); these must be class abilities and not spells

Making a successful Perception check against the tracking Survival check's DC as a move action allows you to add a profane bonus to your Survival check to track someone or something of a good alignment. This bonus is +2 if your prey is neutral good, +5 if chaotic good, and +8 if lawful good.

Verdure Blooded

Your flora-bound ancestory, coupled with your faith in divine powers of nature, make you better able to fight off harmful effects from plants.

Prerequisites: *Nature mystery* (oracle) ᵃ or *plant domain* (cleric, inquisitor ᵃ), and *verdant bloodline* (sorcerer)

You gain a +2 sacred or profane (as appropriate) bonus to Fortitude or Will saving throws against plant-derived agents, such as poisons and alcohols, as well as special abilities from creatures of the plant type requiring Fortitude or Will saving throws.

Vitae Blooded

The glorious purpose of your divine faith is at odds with the touch of the grave within your flesh, empowering you to resist its pull.

Prerequisites: *Glory domain* (cleric, inquisitor ᵃ) or *life mystery* (oracle) ᵃ, and *undead bloodline* (sorcerer)

You gain a +2 sacred or profane (as appropriate) bonus to saving throws versus undead supernatural and special-abilities, and against spells with the death subtype.

Water Blooded

By reaching into the elemental water within your blood, the divinity to which you hold your faith sustains your life against its chosen element.

Prerequisites: *Water domain* (cleric, inquisitor ᵃ) or *wave mystery* (oracle) ᵃ, and *aquatic* ᵃ or *water elemental bloodline* (sorcerer)

You can hold your breath three times as long as normal in water. This does not apply to other situations that may cause for you to hold your breath.

Wind Blooded

The divine voices borne in the wind speak to the elemental air infused into your blood, making navigating the sky seem a natural thing to you.

Prerequisites: *Air domain* (cleric, inquisitor ᵃ) or *wind mystery* (oracle) ᵃ, and *air elemental bloodline* (sorcerer)

You gain a +2 sacred or profane (as appropriate) bonus to Fly skill checks.

Chapter 5

Magic Synergy

By default, spells and magical abilities operate in very specific ways that detail how they will interact with the game world via the provided game mechanics. Little to no leeway is normally permitted regarding how the subsequent results manifest. However, using magic should also be about the players letting their imagination detail how something fantastic can be interpreted into their vision of the game's shaped reality.

Sometimes players will wonder what happens when they try to step beyond these boundaries by mixing their understanding of the real world and tha tof the game, respectively, in unexpected ways. This may include what may happen if two or more spells or magic abilities are used on a target at the same time, or if their magics are otherwise intertwined in some way. Magic Synergy seeks to address these relationships.

Magic Synergy accepts that how the default rules determine magic functions needs to adapt and compromise to suit the circumstances under which that magic is employed. In other words, what is going on around someone who is using magic should influence what the magic is doing. Acknowledging these potential relationships not only makes using magic more dynamic, but also far more interesting and unpredictable because more thought has to go into spell selection and use beyond the default formula.

Magic Synergy also has the benefit of allowing multiple spellcasters to contribute to the Synergy Effect rather than one character possessing all the prerequisites. For instance, a Brittle Magic Synergy Effect allows the fire ef-

Terms of Magic Synergy

Prerequisites: The spell or magic effects that to work together to obtain the desired Magic Synergy Effect.

Synergy Effect: The desired result obtained by using the specified spells or magic effects together.

Magic Synergy and Game Balance

If you are concerned Magic Synergy can introduce a degree of imbalance into your games, you can counter it by requiring each Magic Synergy Effect be purchased as a metamagic feat of the same name. Should you find a separate metamagic feat for each Magic Synergy Effect is too much, you can create single feat, Magic Synergy, with a prerequisite of possessing any spellcasting or spell-like ability. The latter would grant access to all Magic Synergy Effects

fect to come from one spellcaster while the cold can come from another. Two different spellcasters contribute, their combined abilities ensuring the prerequisites are met.

Brittle

Prerequisites: Fire damage spell or effect, cold damage spell or effect

When an object of leather, glass, wood, stone, or any metal is first struck by a damage-causing spell with the fire descriptor and then by a damage-causing spell with the cold descriptor, it may become brittle and vulnerable.

For the object to become brittle, the cold spell must inflict its damage in the same round or the one immediately following the round in which the fire damage is caused. Once this is done, divide the inflicted cold damage by 10 (rounded down.) The result is how much the targeted object's hardness is reduced by, to a minimum of 0 and to a maximum of the fire damage divided by 10 (rounded down.)

The damage tallies from multiple fire and cold attacks inflicted simultaneously stack before dividing by 10, so long as they meet the previously outlined requirements to cause the target object to potentially become brittle. Additional attempts to make the object even more brittle may be attempted, further reducing the hardness value. The reduced hardness remains in effect until the object can be repaired.

5. MAGIC SYNERGY

Magic Synergy Effects

Name	Prerequisites	Synergy Effect
Brittle	Fire damage spell or effect, cold damage spell or effect	The fire and cold make an object brittle, reducing its hardness
Frosted	Cold damage spell or effect, any spell that exposes the subject to water	The cold chills the water, possibly resulting in non-lethal damage and becoming *staggered*
Shocking Surprise	Electricity damage spell or effect, *wall of iron*, *control water*, *control weather*, or the like	Electrify the *wall of iron*, water, et al, effectively turning the electricity damage into an area effect
Shock to the Mind	Three or more charm or compulstion spells or effects in the same round	The target may suffer harm from the rapid succession of mind-affecting influences inflicted upon it
Shock to the System	Three or more transmutation spells or effects that alter the target's shape, appearance, or size used in the same round	The target may suffer harm from the rapid succession of changes inflicted upon it
Steam Flash	Fire damage spell or effect, any spell that exposes the subject to water	The heat turns the water into scalding steam, possibly resulting in nonlethal damage and becoming *fatigued*

For example, a wizard casts fireball *against an iron door (hardness 10), inflicting 33 points of damage once its hardness is accounted for. In the round immediately after, the wizard casts* cone of cold *against the door and inflicts 22 points of damage after accounting for hardness, but he is helped by a white dragon ally whose breath weapon inflicts 24 points of damage (again, accounting for hardness), for a total of 46 cold damage. This causes the door to become brittle and its hardness reduced by 3. Although the total cold damage divided by 10 is 4, the fire damage divided by 10 is 3, capping the hardness reduction at the latter value.*

At the Gamemaster's discretion, other causes of extreme temperature may be substituted for the spell effect, such as alchemist's fire.

Frosted

Prerequisites: Cold damage spell or effect, any spell that exposes the subject to water

By simultaneously exposing a creature to water and cold that is sufficiently chilled to inflict damage (lethal or nonlethal), the subject is placed at risk of suffering additional ill-effects. The target must succeed at an additional Fortitude saving throw versus the cold damage effect's DC or suffer 1d4 additional nonlethal cold damage per die of original cold damage and becomes *staggered*. The *staggered* condition ends when the subject recovers from the nonlethal damage. A subject that is already *staggered* becomes *stunned* instead.

Creatures without a Constitution score are immune to Frosted.

Shocking Surprise

Prerequisites: Electricity damage spell or effect, *wall of iron*, *control water*, *control weather*, or the like

First, cast *wall of iron*, *control water*, *control weather*, or any other spell that creates a pool of water or metal surface you expect your target to touch. Casting a damage-causing spell with the electricity descriptor at the *wall of iron* (et al) or water-covered area conducts the electricity throughout the metal or water surface, effectively transforming the spell's result into an area-effect attack. This area is defined as anywhere on the metal's or water's surface.

Unlike a normal area-effect spell, reduce the damage inflicted by 1d6 per 10 feet a target is away from the point where the electricity spell strikes the metal or water surface, with 0d6 meaning the target is far enough away to feel little more than something comparable to powerful static shock that may break concentration, at best. Similarly, reduce the caster's effective level by 1 for the purpose of spell resistance, when appropriate, per 10 feet from the point of contact.

For example, a 6th-level sorcerer being pursued by orcs casts wall of iron *in a 60 foot long corridor and then tips it over so that it resembles a false floor. After leaving the corridor, the sorcerer waits until the pursuing orcs enter at the other end, at which point he casts a 6d6* lightning bolt *at the corridor's middle, 30 feet away. Because the orcs have just stepped onto the* wall of iron, *they are 30 feet from where the* lightning bolt *strikes, resulting in all orcs in the corridor suffering a 3d6 electricity damage effect from the spell. Also, if any of the orcs have some means*

of spell resistance, the sorcerer would get a +3 caster level bonus to overcome it rather than the usual +6 his level would normally impart.

At the Gamemaster's discretion, causes of electricity damage other than a magic effect may be substituted, such as from natural lighting or a breath weapon.

Shock to the Mind

Prerequisites: Three or more charm or compulstion spells or effects that alter or manipulate the target's thoughts in the same round

Rapid changes to the target's thoughts via effects with the charm or compulstion discriptors can cause confusion and a disconnect from the target's ability to reason, even when the magical effects normally counter each other. If three or more such magical effects target the same subject within the same round there is a chance the manipulations may be too much and harm may result. These effects include the negation of an existing effect that has already altered the target's normal thought process or free will—returning the target's ability to think back to normal is still a change of mental state, after all.

A creature in this situation makes a Will saving throw versus the highest appropriate magical effect's saving throw, +1 for every additional applicable charm or compulsion influence occurring within this timeframe. The creature is *confused* for 1d4 rounds if the save fails. 1d4 points of nonlethal damage per level of the highest level spell affecting the subject's thoughts is also suffered if the saving throw fails by 10 or more.

For example, a Wis 13 cleric casts command *(level 1, DC 12) on a single kobold among an attacking horde. Later in the same round, this kobold is among those targeted by an Int 16 wizard's* mass suggestion *(level 6, DC 19.) Before that round ends it is again targeted by another mind-affecting spell, this time a* rage *spell from one of its allies, an Int 13 kobold wizard (level 3, DC 14.) The kobold must now make a DC 21 (19 + 1 + 1) Will saving throw to resist suffering Shock to the Mind.*

Shock to the System

Prerequisites: Three or more transmutation spells or effects that alter the target's shape, appearance, or size used in the same round

Rapid changes to the target's physiology via transmutation effects can cause the target undue stress, even when the magical effects normally counter each other. If three or more such magical effects target the same subject within the same round there is a chance the stress may be too much and harm may result. These effects include the negation of an existing effect that has altered the target's natural form—changing the target's physiology back to normal is still a physical change, after all.

A creature in this situation makes a Fortitude saving throw versus the highest appropriate magical effect's saving throw, +1 for every additional applicable transmutation effect occurring within this timeframe. The creature is *staggered* and *sickened* for 1d4 rounds if the roll fails. 1d4 points of nonlethal damage per level of the highest level spell inflicting stress upon the subject is also suffered if the saving throw fails by 10 or more.

An object in this situation makes a Fortitude saving throw versus the highest appropriate magical effect's saving throw, +1 for every additional applicable transmutation effect occurring within this timeframe. This saving throw is made even if the object would not normally be allowed a saving throw. In such instances, apply half the object's hardness to the roll as a bonus. 1d4 point of damage per level of the highest level spell inflicting stress upon the subject is suffered if the saving throw fails. Change this to 1d6 points per level if the saving throw fails by 10 or more.

For example, an Int 11 wizard casts reduce person *(level 1, DC 11) on a Cha 12 goblin sorcerer in round one of an encounter, but during its action the goblin counters this by casting* enlarge person *(level 1, DC 12) on itself. Before the round ends, however, yet another wizard with Int 15 uses* polymorph *(level 5, DC 17) on the goblin. The goblin must now make a DC 19 (17 + 1 + 1) Fortitude saving throw to resist suffering Shock to the System.*

Steam Flash

Prerequisites: Fire damage spell or effect, any spell that exposes the subject to water

By simultaneously exposing a creature to flame or heat, and water that is sufficiently hot to inflict damage (lethal or nonlethal) via scalding steam, the subject is placed at risk of suffering additional ill-effects. The target must succeed at an additional Fortitude saving throw versus the fire damage effect's DC or suffer 1d4 additional nonlethal fire damage per die of original fire damage and becomes *fatigued*. The *fatigued* condition ends when the subject recovers from the nonlethal damage. A subject that is already *fatigued* becomes *exhausted* instead.

Creatures without a Constitution score are immune to Steam Flash.

Chapter 6

Craft Synergy

In the core rules, the act of creating an item using the Craft skill is very straightforward. Everything one needs to know about creating a specific item is encapsulated within a single skill, the very skill that is rolled to determine if the process succeeds. Although this simplicity streamlines the process of making something, this system does a disservice to how various areas of knowledge and training may interact with each other during crafting. The concept of Craft Synergy is presented to fill this logical and practical vacuum.

Knowledge represented by other skills, feats, and even class abilities are utilized by Craft Synergy Effects to modify items in ways that reflect their creator's broader capabilities. For example, a character with a certain combat feat may look upon a weapon differently than someone who does not, recognizing through the feat's training ways to create a weapon that better compliments that feat's operation. As a result, they utilize their perspective in the crafting of a mundane weapon, giving it non-magical benefits that allow it to perform differently from the standard of its kind.

Multiple Craft Synergy effects can be applied to the same item simultaneously. To do so, make all the required skill checks with the provided reprecussions for failure coming into effect for all desired Craft Synergy Effects attempted if even one of the skill checks failed. If different Craft Synergy Effects list the same Craft skill, halve the lowest DC modifier(s) (rounded up) and add it (them) to the highest DC modifier.

For example, if adding the Blessed (Craft: armor DC +10) and Parrying (Craft: armor DC +8) Craft Synergy Effects to the same suit of armor, the total modifier would be +14

$$(10 + [8 / 2] = 14.)$$

Terms of Craft Synergy

Prerequisites: The skills, feats, and/or abilities required to work together in order to obtain the desired Craft Synergy Effect. Many Craft Synergy Effects also require the item to which the effect is being applied be of masterwork quality.

Synergy Effect: The desired benefit obtained by using the specified skills, feats, and/or abilities together.

Craft DC: The DC modifier applied to the Craft skill indicated in the prerequisites required to add the Craft Synergy Effect to the appropriate item.

Failure: The results of failing the Craft check to create an item with a Craft Synergy Effect.

Synergy Effect: The results of succeeding at the Craft check to create the item.

Armor Ruining

Your arrow crashes into the enemie's shield, its unusually soft tip crumpling and expanding upon impact, tearing into and fouling the shield's protective surface.

Prerequisites: Greater Sunder, Precise Shot, Skill Focus (Craft: weapons), masterwork ammunition

Craft (weapons) DC: +6

Cost: +15 gp per 10

Failure: The ranged weapon inflicts half damage against all opponents and is incapable of being used to sunder a target. Targets with natural armor, wearing armor, or wielding a shield gain a +1 circumstance bonus to AC against the attack.

The ranged weapon inflicts half damage against most creatures, but inflicts full damage and gains a +2 circumstance damage bonus against constructs or crea-

6. CRAFT SYNERGY

Craft Synergy Effects: Armor and Shields

Name	Prerequisites	Synergy Effect
Blessed	*Channel energy*, Improved Channel, Skill Focus (Craft: armor), masterwork armor	Your *channel energy* DCs gain a +1 bonus
Disarming (armor)	Appropriate Armor Proficiency, Combat Expertise, Improved Disarm, masterwork armor	+1 to disarm and resist disarm attempts
Disarming (shield)	Combat Expertise, Improved Disarm, Shield Focus, Shield Proficiency, masterwork shield	+1 to disarm and resist disarm attempts
Easy Access	Appropriate Armor Proficiency, Skill Focus (Craft: armor), Skill Focus (Profession: tailor), masterwork armor	Getting in and out of armor takes half the normal time
Fireproofed	Appropriate Armor Proficiency, Skill Focus (Craft: alchemy), Spell Focus (evocation) *or* Fire Domain, masterwork armor	+2 to saving throws versus fire and heat
Insulated	Appropriate Armor Proficiency, Skill Focus (Craft: alchemy), Spell Focus (evocation) *or* Water Domain, masterwork armor	+2 to saving throws versus ice and cold
Lightweight (armor)	Appropriate Armor Proficiency, Mobility, Sidestep[a], Skill Focus (Craft: armor), masterwork armor	Reduce weight by 25%, the maximum Dex bonus is 1, and reduce the armor check penalty by 1
Lightweight (shield)	Mobility, Sidestep[a], Shield Proficiency, Skill Focus (Craft: armor), masterwork shield	Reduce weight by 25%, the maximum Dex bonus is 1, and reduce the armor check penalty by 1
Muffled	Skill Focus (Craft: armor), Stealthy, masterwork armor	Reduce the armor check penalty by 2 for sound-based Stealth checks.
Parrying (armor)	Appropriate Armor Proficiency, Defensive Combat Training, masterwork armor	Increase AC bonus from fighting defensively by +2
Parrying (shield)	Defensive Combat Training, Shield Focus, Shield Proficiency, masterwork shield	Increase AC bonus from fighting defensively by +2
Personal (armor)	Alertness, Skill Focus (Craft: armor), Skill Focus (Heal), masterwork armor,	+1 to AC, reduce the armor check penalty by 2
Personal (shield)	Alertness, Skill Focus (Craft: armor), Skill Focus (Heal), masterwork shield	+1 to AC, reduce the armor check penalty by 2
Rager Suit	*Rage*, Skill Focus (Craft: armor), masterwork armor	Gain one free round to a use of *rage* at the cost of an increased armor check penalty and a penalty to concentration checks
Warded	Skill Focus (Craft: armor), Spell Focus (abjuration) *or* Protection Domain, masterwork armor	+1 to saving throws versus magic

[a] See the *Pathfinder® Roleplaying Game: Advanced Player's Guide™*

tures with a natural armor bonus. Consider the attack to have the Greater Sunder feat if made against an opponent wearing armor or wielding a shield. The defender gets to choose which suffers the sundering attack, the armor or the shield if the circumstance does not otherwise indicate a logical choice. Roll for the sunder combat maneuver and its damage separately from the attack's normal damage against the target.

This Craft Synergy Effect may only be applied to piercing ranged weapon ammunition.

Blessed (armor)

Holy symbols and the language of your faith is scrawled into the armor's surface, the materials of which have been mixed with blessed items, such as holy water and relics of your god.

Prerequisites: *Channel energy*, Improved Channel, Skill Focus (Craft: armor), masterwork armor

Craft (armor) DC: +10

Cost: +400 gp

Craft Synergy Effects: Goods

Name	Prerequisites	Synergy Effect
Splash Bottle	Skill Focus (Craft: alchemy), Skill Focus (Craft: glass), Throw Anything, glass bottle or flask	Double splash radius
Terrain Tailored	*Favored terrain*, Skill Focus (cloth), Stealthy, explorer's outfit or traveller's outfit	+2 to Stealth checks in the favored terrain
Thin Pages	Skill Focus (Craft: alchemy), Skill Focus (Craft: books), book or scroll	Increase page count or reduce paper weight
Warmaster's Saddle	*Cavalier's charge*[α] or *mounted archer*[φ], Skill Focus (Craft: leather), Skill Focus (Ride), war saddle	+1d4 damage to a mounted charge attack

[α] See the *Pathfinder® Roleplaying Game: Advanced Player's Guide™*

[φ] See the *Pathfinder® Roleplaying Game: Ultimate Combat™*

Failure: Your *channel energy* DCs suffer a -1 penalty.

Your *channel energy* DCs gain a +1 sacred (or profane) bonus.

Blessed (weapon)

Holy symbols and the language of your faith track across the length and bredth of your weapon. Furthermore, the materials of which it was made have been mixed with holy water, divine relics, and purified by sacred (or profane) rituals at every step.

Prerequisites: *Channel energy*, Improved Channel, Skill Focus (Craft: weapons), masterwork weapon

Craft (weapons) DC: +10

Cost: +400 gp

Failure: The weapon is brittle, reducing its hardness by 2.

The weapon is considered sacred and good (or profane and evil) for the purpose of bypassing damage reduction and the like.

Bloody

Tiny hooks, barbs, coils and the like are built into the weapon's design to better tear the flesh when an opponent is struck, creating a wound that is more likely to continue bleeding. These additions typically make the weapon appear quite malicious and menacing.

Prerequisites: Critical Focus, Bleeding Critical, masterwork piercing or slashing weapon

Craft (weapons) DC: +10

Cost: +100 gp, or +1 gp for ammunition, +200 gp for double weapons (DC 10 saving throw); +200 gp, or +2 gp for ammunition, +400 gp for double weapons (DC 15 saving throw); +300 gp, or +3 gp for ammunition, +600 gp for double weapons (DC 20 saving throw)

Failure: Your target gets a +1 AC bonus against the weapon.

If an opponent suffers damage from your weapon he must then make a Fortitude saving throw or suffer an additional 1d4 points of bleed damage each round on his turn. This bleed damage can be stopped by a DC 15 Heal skill check or through any magical healing. This bleed damage stacks with other bleed damage, including that of previous strikes with a Bloody weapon.

Cleaver

The furthest end of a slashing blade is oversized or otherwise granted additional weight to make it a better weapon for cleaving through multiple foes.

Prerequisites: Appropriate Weapon Proficiency, Cleave, Great Cleave, Power Attack, masterwork slashing weapon

Craft (weapons) DC: +5

Cost: +250gp, +500 gp for double weapons

Failure: The weapon cannot be used for cleaving.

The weapon gains a cumulative +1 damage bonus for every previously cleaved opponent within that same Cleave maneuver.

This cannot be added to ammunition.

6. CRAFT SYNERGY

Craft Synergy Effects: Weapons

Name	Prerequisites	Synergy Effect
Armor Ruining	Greater Sunder, Precise Shot, Skill Focus (Craft: weapons) , masterwork ammunition	Tear into armor, inflicting a sunder attack against a target's armor or shield
Blessed	*Channel energy*, Improved Channel, Skill Focus (Craft: weapons), masterwork weapon	The weapon is sacred and good (or profane and unholy) versus damage reduction
Bloody	Critical Focus, Bleeding Critical, masterwork piercing or slashing weapon	Successfully inflicting damage forces your opponent to make a Fortitude saving throw to resist additional bleed damage
Cleaver	Appropriate Weapon Proficiency, Cleave, Great Cleave, Power Attack, masterwork slashing weapon	+1 cumulative damage for previous successes at cleaving
Disarming (weapon)	Appropriate Weapon Proficiency, Appropriate Weapon Specialization, Combat Expertise, Improved Disarm, masterwork weapon	+1 to disarm and resist disarm attempts
Foe Bane	Favored Enemy (specific), Slayer's Knack [φ], masterwork weapon	+1 to damage and +1 threat range against the favored enemy
Parrying (weapon)	Appropriate Weapon Proficiency, Appropriate Weapon Specialization, Defensive Combat Training, masterwork weapon	Increase AC bonus from fighting defensively by +2
Personal (weapon)	Alertness, Skill Focus (Craft: shield), Skill Focus (Heal), masterwork weapon	Increase the masterwork bonus to attack to +2 and gain a +1 bonus to damage
Sundering	Greater Sunder, Improved Sunder, masterwork weapon	Reduce the targeted item's hardess by 1d4 against a sundering attempt
Tripping	Improved Trip, Tripping Strike [α], masterwork weapon	You are +1 to trip attempts against opponents adjacent to you using the weapon

[α] See the *Pathfinder® Roleplaying Game: Advanced Player's Guide*™

[φ] See the *Pathfinder® Roleplaying Game: Ultimate Combat*™

Disarming

The weapon has curving hooks or gripping notches resembling teeth in the blades and twisting quillians or the like intended to capture an opponent's attacks. Armor or a shield sport hooks intended to do the same.

Prerequisites (armor): Appropriate Armor Proficiency, Combat Expertise, Improved Disarm, masterwork armor

Prerequisites (shield): Combat Expertise, Improved Disarm, Shield Focus, Shield Proficiency, masterwork shield

Prerequisites (weapon): Appropriate Weapon Proficiency, Appropriate Weapon Specialization, Combat Expertise, Improved Disarm, masterwork weapon

Craft (armor or weapons, appropriately) DC: +5 (+8 if armor)

Cost: +75 gp for weapons, +150 gp for double weapons; +125 gp for shields and armor

Failure: The armor or shield's AC bonus is reduced by 1 (to a minimum of no benefit to AC) whereas the weapon is -1 to damage and -1 to disarm.

You receive a +1 bonus to perform the disarm combat maneuver and receive a +1 bonus to your CMD to resist attempts to disarm you of the shield or weapon.

This cannot be added to ammunition.

Easy Access

By adding more clasps and making the armor more reasonably sectioned in a manner that seems more appropriate for clothing rather than armor, less time is needed to get in and out of it.

Prerequisites: Appropriate Armor Proficiency, Skill Focus (Craft: armor), Skill Focus (Profession: tailor), masterwork armor

Craft (armor) DC: +5

Cost: +50%

Failure: The new design is confusing, doubling the time needed to get in and out of the armor.

Halve the time needed to get in and out of armor.

Fireproofed

By treating the armor and adding layers of similarly prepared cloth beneath, the armor and wearer are more resistant to flame.

Prerequisites: Appropriate Armor Proficiency, Skill Focus (Craft: alchemy), Spell Focus (evocation) *or* Fire Domain, masterwork armor

Craft (armor) DC: +8

Cost: +100gp

Failure: The treatment corrodes the armor somewhat, reducing its AC bonus by 1 (to a minimum of no benefit to AC.)

The armor and its wearer gain a +2 circumstance bonus to saving throws versus fire and heat effects.

Foe Bane

By modifying the weapon to accommodate the characteristics of a specific favored enemy, such as designing arrowheads intended to tear up a construct's innards once the surface has been penetrated rather than creating a bleeding wound, the weapon is able to cause more harm against such a foe.

Prerequisites: Favored Enemy (specific), masterwork weapon, Slayer's Knack ᵠ

Craft (weapons) DC: +10

Cost: +200 gp, +4 gp for ammunition; +400 gp for double weapons

Failure: The weapon is -1 to damage against all opponents and it is unable to inflict a critical hit.

The weapon gains a +1 circumstance bonus to damage and an increase of 1 to threat range when used against the *favored enemy* of its creator. However, it is -1 to damage and its threat range is reduced by 1 (to a minimum of 20) against all other foes.

Multiple instances of Foe Bane cannot be applied to the same weapon.

Insulation

By treating the armor and adding layers of similarly prepared cloth beneath, the armor and wearer are more resistant to cold.

Prerequisites: Appropriate Armor Proficiency, Skill Focus (Craft: alchemy), Spell Focus (evocation) *or* Water Domain, masterwork armor

Craft (armor) DC: +8

Cost: +100gp

Failure: The treatment corrodes the armor somewhat, reducing its AC bonus by 1 (to a minimum of no benefit to AC.)

The armor and its wearer gain a +2 circumstance bonus to saving throws versus ice and cold effects.

Lightweight

The armor is noticeably lighter and more accommodating of your movements, making it easier to maneuver about unimpeded.

Prerequisites (armor): Appropriate Armor Proficiency, Mobility, Sidestep ᵃ, Skill Focus (Craft: armor), masterwork armor

Prerequisites (shield): Mobility, Sidestep ᵃ, Shield Proficiency, Skill Focus (Craft: armor), masterwork shield

Craft (armor) DC: +8

Cost: +250 gp

Failure: The armor's AC bonus and maximum dex bonus (if applicable) are both reduced by 1 (possibly resulting in a penalty), and its armor check penalty is increased by 1.

Reduce the armor's or shield's weight by 25% (round up), increase the maximum Dex bonus by 1 (if applicable), and reduce its armor check penalty by 1, to a maximum benefit of no armor check penalty.

Muffled

Fibers carefully intermingled among the armor's moving and noisome sections greatly reduce the sound it makes while worn.

Prerequisites: Skill Focus (Craft: armor), Stealthy, masterwork armor

Craft (armor) DC: +6

Cost: +125 gp

Failure: Increase the armor check penalty by 2 for Dexterity-based skills.

6. Craft Synergy

Reduce the armor check penalty by 2 (to a maximum benefit of 0) regarding sound-based Stealth checks.

Parrying

The weapon has notches in the blades, over-sized, curving quillians, or the like intended to turn and deflect blows. Armor or a shield has hooks, curves, or bulges intended to do the same. Although effective, the design gives the item a somewhat unusual appearance.

Prerequisites (armor): Appropriate Armor Proficiency, Defensive Combat Training, masterwork armor

Prerequisites (shield): Defensive Combat Training, Shield Focus, Shield Proficiency, masterwork shield

Prerequisites (weapon): Appropriate Weapon Proficiency, Appropriate Weapon Specialization, Defensive Combat Training, masterwork weapon

Craft (armor or weapons, appropriately) DC: +5 (+8 if armor)

Cost: +150 gp for weapons, +300 gp for double weapons; +250 gp for shields and armor

Failure: The armor or shield's AC bonus is reduced by 1 (to a minimum of no benefit to AC) whereas the weapon is -2 to damage.

Increase your AC bonus by an additional +2 while fighting defensively. This bonus does not stack from any other Parrying Craft Synergy Effect the character may have applied to his armor, shield, or weapons.

This cannot be added to ammunition.

Personal

Using close observation of the subject's physique, the weapon, armor, or shield has been crafted especially for them and no other. Be it form fitting armor, a shield weighted to be incorporated in the natural flow of the subject's arm, or a weapon the weight and grip of which have been tailor-fit, the item is crafted to compliment one person alone.

Prerequisites (armor): Alertness, Skill Focus (Craft: armor), Skill Focus (Heal), masterwork armor

Prerequisites (shield): Alertness, Skill Focus (Craft: armor), Skill Focus (Heal), masterwork shield

Prerequisites (weapon): Alertness, Skill Focus (Craft: shield), Skill Focus (Heal), masterwork weapon

Craft (armor or weapons, appropriately) DC: +10

Heal DC: 20

Cost: +600 gp for weapons, +1,200 gp for double weapons; +300 gp for shields and armor

Failure: The item works as a regular item of its sort, but reduce its hardness by 2.

Weapons increase their masterwork attack enhancement bonus to +2 and gain a +1 enhancement bonus to damage when wielded by the subject they were personalized for. Armor and shields gain a +1 enhancement bonus to AC and their armor check penalty are lessened by 2. Normally, when used by anyone else the item acts as a normal item of its sort, not even gaining the benefit of the normal masterwork benefits.

Although unlikely, it is possible a personal weapon may be used at its full capabilities by someone else. Someone of the same size category and same creature type (e.g., humanoid) rolls percentile when attempting to do so. On a 01 result they may use the item as though it were their personal item. If they are of a different creature type they roll percentile twice and both results must be 01 to gain these benefits. Similarly, roll percentile an additional time per size category difference between that of the person the item was made for, each also requiring a result of 01.

This cannot be added to ammunition.

Rager Suit

Adding small spikes and the like inside the armor makes it uncomfortable and painful to be dressed in, allowing the wearer's rage to last longer than normal

Prerequisites: *Rage*, Skill Focus (Craft: armor), masterwork armor

Craft (armor) DC: +10

Cost: +50 gp

Failure: The armor check penalty is increased by 1 and the wearer is -4 to concentration checks without any benefits being applied to the wearer's *rage*.

The wearer in a *rage* may do so for an additional free round so long as they spend at least one round from their daily tally first. This bonus round applies to each instance of raging so long as the character is in the armor. However, this comes at a cost of a increase of 1 to the normal armor check penalty and the wearer is -4 to concentration checks.

Splash Glass

Specially designed patterns in the glass bottle you have created ensure the contents splash farther.

Prerequisites: Skill Focus (Craft: alchemy), Skill Focus (Craft: glass), Throw Anything, glass bottle or flask

Craft (glass) DC: +10

Cost: +5 gp

Failure: The bottle or flask does not break properly, resulting in no splash. The contents are only spilled in the 5-foot square of impact.

Double the splash radius of the bottle's or flask's contents.

Sundering

The weapon has had extra weight crafted into its attacking surface in such a way as to increase the force delivered with the attack, improving its chances of destroying another weapon or item struck.

Prerequisites: Greater Sunder, Improved Sunder, masterwork weapon

Craft (weapons) DC: +8

Cost: +80 gp

Failure: The weapon gains the benefits to sundering, but its own hardness suffers twice the penalty applied to its target.

Reduce the targeted item's hardness by 1d4 (roll with each sunder attempt) against the sundering weapon.

This cannot be added to ammunition.

Terrain Tailored

Knowledge of the desired terrain results in superior camouflage being applied to the clothing.

Prerequisites: *Favored terrain*, Skill Focus (cloth), Stealthy, explorer's outfit or traveller's outfit

Craft (cloth) DC: +8

Cost: +15 gp

Failure: Suffer a -2 penalty to Stealth checks in the favored terrain.

Gain a +2 circumstnace bonus to Stealth checks while in the specific *favored terrain* type known to and selected by the creator. Each suit is limited to one *favored terrain* type.

Thin Pages

You may apply a special alchemical treatment to allow a book's pages or a scroll to be thinner—and thus lighter—without losing any resilience or usefulness.

Prerequisites: Skill Focus (Craft: alchemy), Skill Focus (Craft: books), book or scroll

Craft (books) DC: +10

Cost: +25 gp

Failure: The pages are ruined.

A book can either contain twice as many pages without an increase in weight or contain the same amount of pages but weigh half as much. Scrolls weigh half normal.

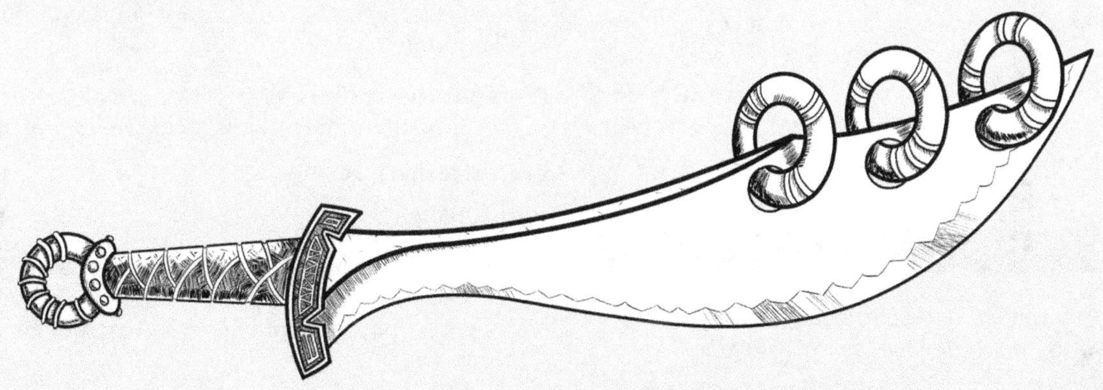

Tripping

By strategically attaching lengths of rope, chain, or the like to a weapon that does not normally affect trip attempts, the weaponc becomes a tool for doing so against nearby targets.

Prerequisites: Improved Trip, Tripping Strike [a], masterwork weapon

Craft (weapons) DC: +5

Cost: +25 gp

Failure: The tripping impliments get in the way, imposing a -1 penalty to all attack rolls.

You gain a +1 circumstance bonus to trip attempts against opponents adjacent to you while wielding the weapon, but you still provoke an attack of opportunity when doing so.

This cannot be added to ammunition or thrown weapons.

Warded

Symbols intended to disipate magic energies are etched into and under the armor's surface.

Prerequisites: Skill Focus (Craft: armor), Spell Focus (abjuration) *or* Protection Domain, masterwork armor

Craft (armor) DC: +10

Cost: +450 gp

Failure: You suffer a -1 penalty saving throws versus all magic effects.

You gain a +1 circumstance bonus to saving throws versus all magic effects. Ignore the harmless annotation to such effects, however. Wearing the armor means you must make a saving throw against all magic effects, even those that are desirable and beneficial.

Warmaster's Saddle

Superior support and design imporves the force delivered by a charge attack from a rider within the saddle.

Prerequisites: *Cavalier's charge* [a] or *mounted archer* [φ], Skill Focus (Craft: leather), Skill Focus (Ride), war saddle

Craft (leather) DC: +6

Cost: +100 gp

Failure: Do not apply the circumstance damage bonus. Instead, the impact from making a mounted charge attack is painful, inflicting 1d8 nonlethal damage upon you.

Apply a +1d4 circumstance damage bonus while making a mounted charge from the saddle.

OPEN GAME LICENSE Version 1.0a

The following text is the property of Wizards of the Coast, Inc. and is Copyright 2000 Wizards of the Coast, Inc ("Wizards"). All Rights Reserved.

1. Definitions: (a)"Contributors" means the copyright and/or trademark owners who have contributed Open Game Content; (b)"Derivative Material" means copyrighted material including derivative works and translations (including into other computer languages), potation, modification, correction, addition, extension, upgrade, improvement, compilation, abridgment or other form in which an existing work may be recast, transformed or adapted; (c) "Distribute" means to reproduce, license, rent, lease, sell, broadcast, publicly display, transmit or otherwise distribute; (d)"Open Game Content" means the game mechanic and includes the methods, procedures, processes and routines to the extent such content does not embody the Product Identity and is an enhancement over the prior art and any additional content clearly identified as Open Game Content by the Contributor, and means any work covered by this License, including translations and derivative works under copyright law, but specifically excludes Product Identity. (e) "Product Identity" means product and product line names, logos and identifying marks including trade dress; artifacts; creatures characters; stories, storylines, plots, thematic elements, dialogue, incidents, language, artwork, symbols, designs, depictions, likenesses, formats, poses, concepts, themes and graphic, photographic and other visual or audio representations; names and descriptions of characters, spells, enchantments, personalities, teams, personas, likenesses and special abilities; places, locations, environments, creatures, equipment, magical or supernatural abilities or effects, logos, symbols, or graphic designs; and any other trademark or registered trademark clearly identified as Product identity by the owner of the Product Identity, and which specifically excludes the Open Game Content; (f) "Trademark" means the logos, names, mark, sign, motto, designs that are used by a Contributor to identify itself or its products or the associated products contributed to the Open Game License by the Contributor (g) "Use", "Used" or "Using" means to use, Distribute, copy, edit, format, modify, translate and otherwise create Derivative Material of Open Game Content. (h) "You" or "Your" means the licensee in terms of this agreement.

2. The License: This License applies to any Open Game Content that contains a notice indicating that the Open Game Content may only be Used under and in terms of this License. You must affix such a notice to any Open Game Content that you Use. No terms may be added to or subtracted from this License except as described by the License itself. No other terms or conditions may be applied to any Open Game Content distributed using this License.

3.Offer and Acceptance: By Using the Open Game Content You indicate Your acceptance of the terms of this License.

4. Grant and Consideration: In consideration for agreeing to use this License, the Contributors grant You a perpetual, worldwide, royalty-free, non-exclusive license with the exact terms of this License to Use, the Open Game Content.

5.Representation of Authority to Contribute: If You are contributing original material as Open Game Content, You represent that Your Contributions are Your original creation and/or You have sufficient rights to grant the rights conveyed by this License.

6.Notice of License Copyright: You must update the COPYRIGHT NOTICE portion of this License to include the exact text of the COPYRIGHT NOTICE of any Open Game Content You are copying, modifying or distributing, and You must add the title, the copyright date, and the copyright holder's name to the COPYRIGHT NOTICE of any original Open Game Content you Distribute.

7. Use of Product Identity: You agree not to Use any Product Identity, including as an indication as to compatibility, except as expressly licensed in another, independent Agreement with the owner of each element of that Product Identity. You agree not to indicate compatibility or co-adaptability with any Trademark or Registered Trademark in conjunction with a work containing Open Game Content except as expressly licensed in another, independent Agreement with the owner of such Trademark or Registered Trademark. The use of any Product Identity in Open Game Content does not constitute a challenge to the ownership of that Product Identity. The owner of any Product Identity used in Open Game Content shall retain all rights, title and interest in and to that Product Identity.

8. Identification: If you distribute Open Game Content You must clearly indicate which portions of the work that you are distributing are Open Game Content.

9. Updating the License: Wizards or its designated Agents may publish updated versions of this License. You may use any authorized version of this License to copy, modify and distribute any Open Game Content originally distributed under any version of this License.

10 Copy of this License: You MUST include a copy of this License with every copy of the Open Game Content You Distribute.

11. Use of Contributor Credits: You may not market or advertise the Open Game Content using the name of any Contributor unless You have written permission from the Contributor to do so.

12 Inability to Comply: If it is impossible for You to comply with any of the terms of this License with respect to some or all of the Open Game Content due to statute, judicial order, or governmental regulation then You may not Use any Open Game Material so affected.

13 Termination: This License will terminate automatically if You fail to comply with all terms herein and fail to cure such breach within 30 days of becoming aware of the breach. All sublicenses shall survive the termination of this License.

14 Reformation: If any provision of this License is held to be unenforceable, such provision shall be reformed only to the extent necessary to make it enforceable.

15 COPYRIGHT NOTICE

Open Game License v 1.0a © 2000, Wizards of the Coast, Inc.

System Reference Document © 2000-2003, Wizards of the Coast, Inc.; Authors Jonathan Tweet, Monte Cook, Skip Williams, Rich Baker, Andy Collins, David Noonan, Rich Redman, Bruce R. Cordell, based on original material by E. Gary Gygax and Dave Arneson.

Modern System Reference Document © 2002, Wizards of the Coast, Inc.; Authors Bill Slavicsek, Jeff Grubb, Rich Redman, Charles Ryan, based on material by Jonathan Tweet, Monte Cook, Skip Williams, Richard Baker, Peter Adkison, Bruce R. Cordell, John Tynes, Andy Collins, and JD Wiker.

Anger of Angels. © 2003, Sean K. Reynolds.

Book of Fiends. © 2003, Green Ronin Publishing; Authors: Aaron Loeb, Erik Mona, Chris Pramas, Robert J. Schwalb.

The Book of Hallowed Might. © 2003, Monte J. Cook.

Monte Cook's Arcana Unearthed. © 2003, Monte J. Cook.

Path of the Magi. © 2002 Citizen Games/ Troll Lord Games; Authors: Mike Mcartor, W. Jason Peck, Jeff Quick, and Sean K. Reynolds.

Skreyn's Register: The Bonds of Magic. © 2002, Sean K. Reynolds.

Angel, Monadic Deva from *The Tome of Horrors, Revised.* © 2002, Necromancer Games, Inc.; Author: Scott Greene, based on original material by E. Gary Gygax.

Angel, Movanic Deva from *The Tome of Horrors, Revised.* © 2002, Necromancer Games, Inc.; Author: Scott Greene, based on original material by E. Gary Gygax.

Brownie from *The Tome of Horrors, Revised.* © 2002, Necromancer Games, Inc.; Author: Scott Greene, based on original material by E. Gary Gygax.

Daemon, Ceustodaemon (Guardian Daemon) from *The Tome of Horrors, Revised.* © 2002, Necromancer Games, Inc.; Author: Scott Greene, based on original material by E. Gary Gygax.

Daemon, Derghodaemon from *The Tome of Horrors, Revised.* © 2002, Necromancer Games, Inc.; Author: Scott Greene, based on original material by E. Gary Gygax.

Daemon, Hydrodaemon from *The Tome of Horrors, Revised.* © 2002, Necromancer Games, Inc.; Author: Scott Greene, based on original material by E. Gary Gygax.

Daemon, Piscodaemon from *The Tome of Horrors, Revised.* © 2002, Necromancer Games, Inc.; Author: Scott Greene, based on original material by E. Gary Gygax.

Froghemoth from *The Tome of Horrors, Revised.* © 2002, Necromancer Games, Inc.; Author: Scott Greene, based on original material by E. Gary Gygax.

Ice Golem from *The Tome of Horrors, Revised.* © 2002, Necromancer Games, Inc.; Author: Scott Greene, based on original material by E. Gary Gygax.

Iron Cobra from *The Tome of Horrors, Revised.* © 2002, Necromancer Games, Inc.; Author: Scott Greene, based on original material by E. Gary Gygax.

Marid from *The Tome of Horrors, Revised.* © 2002, Necromancer Games, Inc.; Author: Scott Greene, based on original material by E. Gary Gygax.

Mihstu from *The Tome of Horrors, Revised.* © 2002, Necromancer Games, Inc.; Author: Scott Greene, based on original material by E. Gary Gygax.

Nabasu Demon from *The Tome of Horrors, Revised.* © 2002, Necromancer Games, Inc.; Author: Scott Greene, based on original material by E. Gary Gygax.

Necrophidius from *The Tome of Horrors, Revised.* © 2002, Necromancer Games, Inc.; Author: Scott Greene, based on original material by E. Gary Gygax.

Sandman from *The Tome of Horrors, Revised.* © 2002, Necromancer Games, Inc.; Author: Scott Greene, based on original material by E. Gary Gygax.

Scarecrow from *The Tome of Horrors, Revised.* © 2002, Necromancer Games, Inc.; Author: Scott Greene, based on original material by E. Gary Gygax.

Shadow Demon from *The Tome of Horrors, Revised.* © 2002, Necromancer Games, Inc.; Author: Scott Greene, based on original material by E. Gary Gygax.

Wood Golem from *The Tome of Horrors, Revised.* © 2002, Necromancer Games, Inc.; Author: Scott Greene, based on original material by E. Gary Gygax.

The Book of Experimental Might. © 2008, Monte J. Cook. All rights reserved.

Tome of Horrors. © 2002, Necromancer Games, Inc.; Authors: Scott Greene, with Clark Peterson, Erica Balsley, Kevin Baase, Casey Christofferson, Lance Hawvermale, Travis Hawvermale, Patrick Lawinger, and Bill Webb; Based on original content from TSR.

Conan the Roleplaying Game. © 2003 Conan Properties International LLC.

Sword of our Fathers © 2003. The Game Mechanics.

Mutants and Masterminds © 2002, Green Ronin Publishing.

Unearthed Arcana © 2004, Wizards of the Coast, Inc.; Andy Collins, Jesse Decker, David Noonan, Rich Redman.

OGL Barbarian: The Deep Wilder © 2005; Author Steven Trustrum, Misfit Studios.

OGL Barbarian: The Sea Devil © 2005; Author Steven Trustrum, Misfit Studios.

OGL Barbarian: The Hawkeye © 2005; Author Steven Trustrum, Misfit Studios.

OGL Barbarian: The Barbaric Warrior © 2005; Author Steven Trustrum, Misfit Studios.

OGL Barbarian: Barbaric Treasures © 2005; Author Steven Trustrum, Misfit Studios.

Hyboria's Fiercest: Barbarians, Borderers & Nomads. © 2005 Conan Properties International LLC.

Pathfinder RPG Core Rulebook. © 2009, Paizo Inc.; Author: Jason Bulmahn, based on material by Jonathan Tweet, Monte Cook, and Skip Williams.

Advanced Player's Guide. © 2010, Paizo Inc.; Author: Jason Bulmahn.

Pathfinder Roleplaying Game Ultimate Magic. © 2011, Paizo Inc.; Authors: Jason Bulmahn, Tim Hitchcock, Colin McComb, Rob McCreary, Jason Nelson, Stephen Radney-MacFarland, Sean K Reynolds, Owen K.C. Stephens, and Russ Taylor.

Pathfinder Roleplaying Game Ultimate Combat. © 2011. Paizo Inc.; Authors: Jason Bulmahn, Tim Hitchcock, Colin McComb, Rob McCreary, Jason Nelson, Stephen Radney-MacFarland, Sean K. Reynolds, Owen K.C. Stephens, and Russ Taylor.

Superior Synergy. ©2005 Misfit Studios. Author Steven Trustrum.

Superior Synergy: Fantasy PFRPG Edition. © 2012 Misfit Studios. Author Steven Trustrum.

Skill Synergy Effects

Qualified?	Primary Skill	Synergy Skill	Synergy Effect
	Appraise	Craft (various)	Assess Item
		Craft (various)	Reconsider Assessment
	Bluff	Acrobatics	Twisting Feint
		Intimidate	Bluster
		Linguistics	Twisting Words
	Climb	Acrobatics	Like a Monkey
	Craft (alchemy)	Knowledge (nature)	Prime Ingredient
	Craft (carpentry)	Knowledge (engineering)	Measure Twice, Cut Once
	Craft (stonemasonry)	Knowledge (engineering)	Measure Twice, Chisel Once
	Craft (traps)	Craft (carpentry)	Dangerous Woodcraft
		Craft (stonemasonry)	Perilous Stonework
		Stealth	Know How to Hide It
	Diplomacy	Bluff	Silver Tongued
		Knowledge (various)	Travel in the Same Circles
		Sense Motive	Discern Meaning
	Disable Device	Craft (locks)	Locksmith
		Craft (traps)	Trap Springer
		Craft (various)	Tear It Down
	Disguise	Bluff	Sell the Story
		Perform (act)	Become the Role
	Escape Artist	Acrobatics	Hard to Hold
		Sleight of Hand	Slip the Knot
	Fly	Acrobatics	Aerobatics
	Heal	Knowledge (nature)	Nature's Remedy
	Intimidate	Bluff	Do It or Else!
		Bluff	Fear Me!
	Knowledge (nature)	Survival	Know the Wilds
	Perception	Knowledge (engineering)	Locate the Hidden
		Sense Motive	Something's Not Right
	Perform (comedy)	Acrobatics	Slapstick
	Perform (dance)	Acrobatics	Surprise Moves
	Profession (various)	Knowledge (various)	In the Know
	Ride	Handle Animal	Know Your Mount
	Sense Motive	Diplomacy	Spot the Tell
		Perception	Gut Feeling
		Perception	Wink, Wink, Say No More
		Spellcraft	See the Signs
	Sleight of Hand	Bluff	Confident Facade
	Spellcraft	Knowledge (arcana)	Lore of Mysteries
		Use Magic Device	Scroll Reader
	Survival	Knowledge (dungeoneering)	Tunnel Rat
		Knowledge (geography)	Lay of the Land
		Knowledge (nature)	Wilderness Awareness
		Knowledge (planes)	Otherworldly Awareness
		Perception	Spot the Trail
	Use Magic Device	Linguistics	Read Spell Scroll
		Spellcraft	Decrypt Scroll

Feat Synergy Effects

Qualified?	Name	Prerequisites
	Adamantine Lungs	Athletic, Endurance, Great Fortitude
	Appealing Leader	Leadership, Persuasive, Sociable α, Voice of the Sibyl μ
	Archer's Wall	Missile Shield α, Point-Blank Shot, Precise Shot, Shield Focus, Shield Proficiency
	Avoid Sneak Attack	Acrobatic, Alertness, Lightning Reflexes
	Bait and Strike	Combat Expertise, Deceptive, Disengaging Feint φ, Improved Feint
	Block and Counter	Combat Expertise, Combat Reflexes, Weapon Specialisation, and Improved Disarm or Improved Trip
	Body Flip	Athletic, Improved Grapple, Improved Trip
	Chosen Weapon	Greater Weapon Focus, Power Attack, Weapon Focus, Weapon Specialization
	Clear Some Space	Combat Expertise, Dodge, Improved Disarm, Mobility, Spring Attack, Whirlwind Attack
	Confined Trick Attack	Acrobatics, Acrobatic Steps, Nimble Moves, Step Up
	Countercharge	Mobility, Run, Step-Up
	Desperate Dodge	Acrobatic, Agile Maneuvers, Dodge
	Distraction	Deft Hands, Persuasive
	Dive for Cover	Improved Initiative, Lightning Reflexes, Quick Draw
	Enduring Swimmer	Athletic, Endurance, Skill Focus (Swim)
	Guarded Caster	Combat Casting, Spell Focus, Spell Mastery
	Headsman's Stroke	Combat Expertise, Combat Reflexes, Critical Focus, Vital Strike
	Heave	Athletic, Great Fortitude, Toughness
	High Diver	Acrobatic, Athletic, Skill Focus (Swim)
	Leaping Lunge	Acrobatic, Lunge, Power Attack
	Limber Wrestler	Acrobatic, Dodge, Improved Unarmed Strike, Improved Grapple, Mobility
	Low Charge	Charge Through α, Dodge, Mobility, Power Attack
	Open Defense	Combat Reflexes, Deceitful, Improved Feint
	Oversized Mount	Acrobatic, Animal Affinity, Athletic
	Oversized Rush	Improved Bull Rush, Improved Grapple, Improved Unarmed Strike, Power Attack
	Rampaging Whirlwind	Acrobatic, Combat Expertise, Combat Reflexes, Dodge, Mobility, Spring Attack, Whirlwind Attack
	Ranged Disarm	Combat Expertise, Improved Disarm, Improved Precise Shot, Point-Blank Shot, Precise Shot
	Ritualize Spell	Maximize Spell, Skill Focus (Knowledge: Arcana), Skill Focus (Spellcraft), Spell Focus
	Rolling Rider	Acrobatic, Animal Affinity
	Second Guess	Alertness, Deceitful, Persuasive
	Shield Rush	Improved Bull Rush, Improved Shield Bash, Power Attack, Shield Proficiency
	Staggering Blow	Bludgeoner φ, Dazing Assault α, Weapon Focus
	Steady Step	Acrobatic, Acrobatic Steps, Nimble Moves
	Stop Charge	Deadly Aim, Vital Strike, Weapon Focus
	Sure Grip	Acrobatic, Athletic, Skill Focus (Climb)
	Swinging Attack	Athletic, Combat Expertise, Nimble Moves
	Treasonous Dodge	Agile Maneuvers, Dodge, Flanking Foil φ, Mobility, Spring Attack
	Vault Opponent	Acrobatic, Agile Maneuvers, Sidestep α, Step Up
	Whirling Deflection	Combat Reflexes, Deflect Arrows, Improved Unarmed Strike, Lightning Reflexes
	Whirling Return	Combat Reflexes, Deflect Arrows, Improved Unarmed Strike, Lightning Reflexes, Snatch Arrows
	Whistling Shot	Alertness, Blind-Fight, Improved Blind-Fight α

Class Synergy Effects

Qualified?	Name	Prerequisites
	Agile Stride	*Trackless step, travel domain, woodland stride*
	Ambush Strike	*Favored terrain, sneak attack*
	Arcane Alchemy	*Alchemy**, arcane spells*
	Arcane Blooded	*Arcane bloodline, magic domain*
	Ballad of Ire	*Bardic performance: dirge of doom, favored enemy, rage*
	Bardic Blood	*Bardic perforamcne, maestro bloodline*ᵘ
	Beast Walker	*Animal domain, wild shape*
	Blessed Arcana	Arcane spells, *magic domain*
	Blessed Fury	*Chaos domain, rage,* and *battle mystery** or *war domain*
	Bushwhack	*Dead shot deed*ᵠ, *sneak attack, targeting deed*ᵠ
	Challenge of Hatred	*Challenge**ᵠ, and *smite evil* or *smite good** or *favored enemy*
	Channel Rage	*Channel energy, rage*
	Chaos Blooded	*Chaos domain, aberrant bloodline*
	Cruel Performance	*Bardic performance, cruelty**, *touch of corruption**
	Damned Companion	*Touch of corruption**, and an animal/creature companion class ability
	Dance of Fists	*Bardic performance, flurry of blows*
	Dancing Roll	*Versatile performance, defensive roll*
	Divine Companion	Divine spells, and a class ability that creates a close bond to an animal, object, or creature
	Divine Knowledge	*Knowledge domain* or *lore mystery**, *bardic knowledge* or *lore*
	Evil's Select	*Evil domain, smite good**
	Favored Commander	*Inspiring command**, and *battle mystery** or *war domain*
	Favored Monster	*Favored enemy, monster lore**
	Favored Stride	*Favored terrain, trackless step, woodland stride*
	Flame Blooded	*Fire domain* or *flame mystery**, and *fire elemental bloodline*
	Furious Smite Evil	*Rage, smite evil*
	Furious Smite Good	*Rage, smite good**
	Good's Select	*Good domain, smite evil*
	Grotesque Beast	*Mutagen**, *wild shape*
	Hallowed Terrain	*Terrain mastery**, *travel domain*
	Holy Companion	*Lay on hands,* and an animal/creature companion class ability
	Honorable Defense	*Defensive stance**, *honorable stand*ᵠ
	Hymnal Channeling	*Bardic performance, channel energy*
	Liquid Rage	*Alchemy**, *mutagen**, *rage*
	Merciful Performance	*Bardic performance, lay on hands, mercy*
	Performing Companion	*Bardic performance,* an animal/creature companion class ability
	Quivering Performance	*Bardic performance, quivering palm*
	Raging Companion	Rage, an animal/creature companion class ability
	Raging Performance	*Bardic performance, rage*
	Raging Spell	Arcane spells, *rage*
	Sacred Deception	Any *advanced rogue talent, trickery domain*
	Sacred Shield	*Defensive stance**, *protection domain*

Class Synergy Effects, Continued

Qualified?	Name	Prerequisites
	Safe Terrain	*Evasion, favored terrain, trap sense*
	Shadow-Shrouded	*Darkness domain*, and *shadow illusion* or *shadow bloodline*^α
	Showboat	*Bardic performance*, any *deeds*^ϙ
	Sneaky Companion	*Rogue talent* or *ninja trick*^ϙ, and an animal/creature companion class ability
	Stone Blooded	*Earth domain* or *stone mystery*^α, and *deep earth*^α or *earth elemental bloodline*
	Stunning Performance	*Bardic performance, ki pool, stunning fist* (requires the ability, not the feat)
	Tomb Blooded	*Bones mystery*^α or *death domain*, and *undead bloodline*
	Track Evil	*Detect evil, track*; these must be class abilities and not spells
	Track Good	*Detect good*^α, *track*; these must be class abilities and not spells
	Vendure Blooded	*Nature mystery*^α or *plant domain*, and *verdant bloodline*^α
	Vitae Blooded	*Glory domain* or *life mystery*^α, and *undead bloodline*
	Water Blooded	*Water domain* or *wave mystery*^α, and *aquatic*^α or *water elemental bloodline*
	Wind Blooded	*Air domain* or *wind mystery*^α, and *air elemental bloodline*

Magic Synergy Effects

Qualified?	Name	Prerequisites
	Brittle	Fire damage spell or effect, cold damage spell or effect
	Frosted	Cold damage spell or effect, any spell that exposes the subject to water
	Shocking Surprise	Electricity damage spell or effect, *wall of iron, control water, control weather*, or the like
	Shock to the Mind	Three or more charm or compulstion spells or effects in the same round
	Shock to the System	Three or more transmutation spells or effects that alter the target's shape, appearance, or size used in the same round
	Steam Flash	Fire damage spell or effect, any spell that exposes the subject to water

Craft Synergy Effects: Armor and Shields

Qualified?	Name	Prerequisites
	Blessed	*Channel energy*, Improved Channel, Skill Focus (Craft: armor), masterwork armor
	Disarming (armor)	Appropriate Armor Proficiency, Combat Expertise, Improved Disarm, masterwork armor
	Disarming (shield)	Combat Expertise, Improved Disarm, Shield Focus, Shield Proficiency, masterwork shield
	Easy Access	Appropriate Armor Proficiency, Skill Focus (Craft: armor), Skill Focus (Profession: tailor), masterwork armor
	Fireproofed	Appropriate Armor Proficiency, Skill Focus (Craft: alchemy), Spell Focus (evocation) *or* Fire Domain, masterwork armor
	Insulated	Appropriate Armor Proficiency, Skill Focus (Craft: alchemy), Spell Focus (evocation) *or* Water Domain, masterwork armor
	Lightweight (armor)	Appropriate Armor Proficiency, Mobility, Sidestep^α, Skill Focus (Craft: armor), masterwork armor
	Lightweight (shield)	Mobility, Sidestep^α, Shield Proficiency, Skill Focus (Craft: armor), masterwork shield
	Muffled	Skill Focus (Craft: armor), Stealthy, masterwork armor
	Parrying (armor)	Appropriate Armor Proficiency, Defensive Combat Training, masterwork armor
	Parrying (shield)	Defensive Combat Training, Shield Focus, Shield Proficiency, masterwork shield
	Personal (armor)	Alertness, Skill Focus (Craft: armor), Skill Focus (Heal), masterwork armor,
	Personal (shield)	Alertness, Skill Focus (Craft: armor), Skill Focus (Heal), masterwork shield
	Rager Suit	*Rage*, Skill Focus (Craft: armor), masterwork armor
	Warded	Skill Focus (Craft: armor), Spell Focus (abjuration) *or* Protection Domain, masterwork armor

Craft Synergy Effects: Goods

Qualified?	Name	Prerequisites
	Splash Bottle	Skill Focus (Craft: alchemy), Skill Focus (Craft: glass), Throw Anything, glass bottle or flask
	Terrain Tailored	*Favored terrain*, Skill Focus (cloth), Stealthy, explorer's outfit or traveller's outfit
	Thin Pages	Skill Focus (Craft: alchemy), Skill Focus (Craft: books), book or scroll
	Warmaster's Saddle	*Cavalier's charge*[α] or *mounted archer*[φ], Skill Focus (Craft: leather), Skill Focus (Ride), war saddle

Craft Synergy Effects: Weapons

Qualified?	Name	Prerequisites
	Armor Ruining	Greater Sunder, Precise Shot, Skill Focus (Craft: weapons), masterwork ammunition
	Blessed	*Channel energy*, Improved Channel, Skill Focus (Craft: weapons), masterwork weapon
	Bloody	Critical Focus, Bleeding Critical, masterwork piercing or slashing weapon
	Cleaver	Appropriate Weapon Proficiency, Cleave, Great Cleave, Power Attack, masterwork slashing weapon
	Disarming (weapon)	Appropriate Weapon Proficiency, Appropriate Weapon Specialization, Combat Expertise, Improved Disarm, masterwork weapon
	Foe Bane	Favored Enemy (specific), Slayer's Knack[φ], masterwork weapon
	Parrying (weapon)	Appropriate Weapon Proficiency, Appropriate Weapon Specialization, Defensive Combat Training, masterwork weapon
	Personal (weapon)	Alertness, Skill Focus (Craft: shield), Skill Focus (Heal), masterwork weapon
	Sundering	Greater Sunder, Improved Sunder, masterwork weapon
	Tripping	Improved Trip, Tripping Strike[α], masterwork weapon